ASCENDING SHADOWS

Unraveling the Secrets of the 23ᵈ Floor

ECHO SABLE

Table of Contents

Chapter 1

The Ever-Rising Elevator

The story unfolds in a rapidly developing, extremely crowded metropolis.

In such burgeoning cities, a defining characteristic emerges: as the population swells, buildings rise skyward to accommodate the masses. These towering structures are known as skyscrapers.

In these urban jungles, commerce thrives to an extraordinary degree. A diverse array of businesses flourishes, with many forming large conglomerates. Those employed by these institutions enjoy stable jobs and considerable incomes, forming a demographic known as the middle class.

In these sprawling metropolises, every inch of land is incredibly valuable, and rent prices soar to astronomical heights. Even the middle class, with their fixed and stable incomes, find such costs prohibitively expensive.

As a result, the dream of owning a residential unit becomes a cherished aspiration for many with steady employment.

Jude Bailey was one such dreamer. As a director in a vast corporate machine, his life was a tapestry woven with the certainty of routine and the comfort of predictability. His evenings were spent poring over architectural blueprints, his imagination constructing futures from lines and angles. The newspaper advertisements, promising visions of new beginnings, were his nightly companions.

On a sweltering Saturday, Jude Bailey's anticipation was palpable. The morning paper had announced the completion of a new skyscraper, its units within reach, both financially and physically. The building promised panoramic views of the city, its expansive balconies teasing the notion of endless possibilities. With the sun blazing overhead, Jude Bailey ascended the hills in his car, his heart matching the rhythm of the engine's purr.

There it stood, a majestic sentinel against the sky, the 27-story edifice that seemed to challenge the very laws of gravity. Jude Bailey marveled at the architectural precision, the seamless alignment of concrete and steel, each floor a testament to human ingenuity and the audacity to reach higher.

As he parked at the foot of the tower, the scent of fresh construction greeted him—a heady mix of paint and plaster, of dreams solidifying into reality. To others, it might have been merely a scent, but to Jude Bailey, it was the intoxicating aroma of potential.

He crossed the threshold into the lobby, where grand glass doors, still veiled in a thin film of dust, awaited their first polish. On the glass, cryptic symbols and swirls of white powder whispered secrets yet to be discovered. The building was a blank canvas, and Jude Bailey was ready to paint his future upon it.

The lobby floor was crafted from artificial marble, and one wall boasted a vibrant mosaic of colorful tiles. On the opposite wall, rows of stainless steel mailboxes gleamed under the ambient lighting.

Jude Bailey pondered the grandeur of the building. It could certainly be considered first-class. Once inhabited, the addition of a few pots of flowers and plants in the lobby would undoubtedly enhance its impressive appearance.

Standing in the lobby, Jude Bailey imagined himself as an owner, meticulously examining a chipped tile.

Minutes passed before he realized there seemed to be no one else in the building. Of course, the inhabitants were yet to arrive, but where was the guardian of this edifice?

With a decisive rap on the mailbox, he shattered the silence.

Eventually, a man emerged from the shadows of the stairwell. He was tall and angular, his diminutive eyes darting suspiciously beneath heavy lids. "May I help you?" he demanded, his voice a gravelly drawl.

Jude Bailey puffed his chest, asserting, "I'm here to see the house."

The man's demeanor softened, albeit slightly, as he produced a jangling cluster of keys. "Which unit?"

Jude Bailey, resolute in his choice, replied, "Something high, above the 20th floor, but not the top—it gets too hot."

The man's eyes rolled with indifference as he handed over two keys. "23rd floor. Take a look yourself."

This was unprecedented for Jude Bailey, who was accustomed to the hovering presence of agents or managers. Yet, he relished the autonomy; it afforded him the luxury of scrutiny without the constraints of politeness. Purchasing a home demanded the utmost care, the investment of a lifetime. Alone, he could inspect every corner to his satisfaction.

He watched the thin man retreat up the stairs and approached the elevator, pressing the button that summoned it with a mechanical chime. Inside, the walls were a sleek expanse of aluminum, reflecting his thoughts as he ascended.

As the elevator glided upward, Jude Bailey's imagination raced ahead. Visions of a life unfettered by rent payments, surrounded by luxury, consumed him. He pictured the balcony, a perch from which he could sip whiskey and survey the city below. If the place met his expectations, his family would surely adore it as well.

Engrossed in these dreams, time seemed to elongate. He glanced at the panel of floor numbers, expecting the familiar glow of progress, but none were illuminated.

A frown creased his brow. Likely a loose wire, he mused, resolving to mention it to the manager later. Still, he felt the steady ascent, unwavering and sure.

After all, the 23nd floor was a lofty aspiration, and even the swiftest of elevators required its due time.

Jude Bailey was in a relaxed mood, whistling a popular tune. But as the final note faded, the elevator hadn't stopped yet. He could feel it still ascending.

After a moment, Jude Bailey reached out and slapped the elevator door. He knew it wouldn't open while the elevator was moving, but he'd been in there for far too long.

Even by the 23nd floor, he should have arrived by now. He pressed several buttons in succession, but it was useless. The elevator kept climbing, and he could feel it.

Anxiety began to creep in, but Jude Bailey quickly found it amusing. If the elevator stopped moving, it wouldn't be a big problem. But where could it go if it kept rising? At most, it would reach the top floor and stop. Would it emerge from the roof and fly into the sky?

The absurdity of the notion tugged a laugh from his lips, but the humor was short-lived. The elevator's relentless climb persisted, the minutes stretching into an eternity. He twisted the keys in his hand, eyes fixed on the unlit panel of numbers that stubbornly refused to betray their secrets.

Laughter turned to silence, and silence to dread. Five minutes, perhaps more, had slipped by with no sign of respite. Perspiration beaded on his forehead, trickling down his back as he jabbed repeatedly at the buttons, desperation mounting with each futile press.

The elevator was cool, yet Jude Bailey was drenched, his shirt clinging to his skin. He hammered at the door, fingers mashing the "alarm" and "stop" buttons in a frantic litany. But the elevator, it seemed, had a will of its own, continuing its inexorable rise.

Logic dictated that such an elevation was impossible; no skyscraper breached the heavens to such heights. The building was capped at 36 floors, a mere fraction of the distance they seemed to have traveled. Perhaps the machinery had faltered, leaving him stranded mid-journey, a temporary inconvenience that would surely be rectified.

The small-eyed administrator would notice his absence, wouldn't he? Realizing the elevator's plight, he would summon assistance, and Jude Bailey would emerge unscathed.

Yet, beneath the veneer of rationality, Jude Bailey knew with bone-deep certainty: the elevator was still rising.

Despite the smooth ascent, a sensation of movement persisted, undeniable in its subtlety. As the seconds ticked by, fear morphed into terror, a visceral dread that clawed at the edges of his sanity. What destination awaited him at the terminus of this inexplicable journey?

Panic surged, culminating in a scream that tore from his throat, echoing wildly within the confines of the elevator. And then, as abruptly as it had begun, the ascent ceased. The elevator shuddered, then stilled, its doors sliding open with an unceremonious hiss.

Jude Bailey staggered out, heart pounding in his chest, and clutched the wall for support. Before him stretched a hallway, flanked by doors that stood like sentinels on either side. The elevator door remained open, grounding him in the confines of the building and anchoring him to reality.

He reached out to wipe away his sweat, finding nothing amiss. Everything that had just happened felt like a nightmare, and Jude Bailey couldn't comprehend what was going on. He had to rationalize it: the elevator must have stopped halfway, otherwise, he wouldn't have been in there for so long.

The keys in his hand served as a tangible reminder that he was not dreaming—his mission to explore the residential unit remained unchanged.

With determination, he approached the doors lining the hallway. Selecting a key, he inserted it into the lock, the click of the tumblers aligning a reassuring sound in the silence. As the door swung open, the scent of fresh paint and new beginnings washed over him. The corridor led him into a spacious living room, a balcony promising vistas beyond.

Joy surged within him as he crossed the threshold, the door whispering shut behind him. The expanse of the living room delighted him, and he moved eagerly towards the glass doors that led to the balcony.

But as he stepped outside, he was stunned. In that moment, the world shifted. When he arrived, the sun had been shining brightly, the road gleaming with scorching reflections. Now, standing on the balcony, all he saw was a gray expanse with no visibility.

When had the weather turned bad?

The vibrant sunlit street had vanished, replaced by an oppressive gray void that swallowed the horizon. His heart lurched. Where once there was solid ground, now there was nothing — no comforting solidity beneath him, just an endless, swirling mist.

Panic clawed at his chest as he leaned over the railing, eyes wide with disbelief. The residential unit seemed to be adrift, suspended in a nebulous expanse with no sky above, no earth below. It was as if he had stepped into another realm, the laws of reality rewritten.

A scream tore from his lips, a primal sound of terror. Stumbling backwards, he collided with the glass door, the impact sending him sprawling into the living room. His voice faltered, reduced to a strangled gasp as he scrambled to his feet, mind racing with confusion.

Fleeing to the hallway, he flung open the door and dashed towards the waiting elevator, only to hesitate at its brink. The thought of returning to that confining box was unbearable. He needed to escape, to find someone, anyone, who could explain this madness.

Yet as he searched for the stairwell, a dawning horror gripped him. His legs trembled, refusing to carry him further. There were no stairs—no emergency exit, no means of descent. The building, it seemed, defied convention, trapping him in its enigmatic embrace.

Jude Bailey clearly recalled the staircase, the path taken by the small-eyed administrator who descended from above. Yet now, in his frantic search, the stairs had vanished, leaving him trapped in a building that defied logic. His mind reeled, disoriented by the impossibility of a structure without stairs.

Jude Bailey stood frozen, his mind a tumult of fear and disbelief. How had the mundane transformed into the extraordinary? How could a simple viewing become a journey into the unknown? As shadows closed in around him, he realized he was caught in a mystery beyond his comprehension, a narrative that defied the boundaries of logic and reason.

Desperation fueled his erratic sprint through the hallway, but every turn yielded only blank walls and the gaping maw of the elevator doors, beckoning him into their metallic embrace. It was as if the building itself conspired against him, a sentient entity with its own sinister agenda. He had no choice; the elevator was his only means of escape.

With a heart pounding in his chest, Jude Bailey stumbled into the elevator, jabbing the button with trembling fingers. As the doors slid shut and the descent began, he succumbed to an overwhelming tide of emotion. Tears flowed unchecked, a visceral response to the terror that had pushed him to the brink.

His legs threatened to give way, forcing him to clutch the elevator's interior for support. The sensation of movement beneath his feet was both a relief and a trigger for the release of his pent-up screams.

The elevator shuddered to a halt, its doors parting to reveal the familiar lobby.

Jude Bailey burst forth, colliding with the row of mailboxes in a cacophony of sound. Gasping for breath, he surveyed his surroundings, eyes alighting on the glass doors that framed the outside world. The ground was solid beneath him, and the street beyond teemed with life.

A hand clamped down on his shoulder, and Jude Bailey spun around, nerves aflame with the anticipation of more horrors. It was the administrator, his eyes disconcertingly small, his smile twisted into a parody of warmth. "Sir, Are you satisfied?" the man inquired, his voice dripping with malice.

Panic surged anew, and Jude Bailey screamed, shoving the administrator aside with such force that the man sprawled to the ground. Unheeding of the consequences, he fled, the administrator's shouts fading into the background as he dashed to his car. His hands fumbled with the keys, the engine roaring to life as he sped away, the intersection looming ahead.

The blare of an oncoming car's horn shattered the air, a piercing warning that went unheeded. Impact came with a shattering force, metal crumpling in a symphony of destruction. A scream, a flash of pain, and then darkness as Jude Bailey was hurled into unconsciousness.

In the aftermath, Jude Bailey found himself in a hospital bed, recounting the impossible events to those who would listen.

The building's manager, Rory, became a focal point for questions.

A seasoned hand in the world of property management, Rory was accustomed to the ebb and flow of prospective buyers. The building, a new addition to the cityscape, remained uninhabited, yet drew a steady stream of interest.

Recalling the day's events, Rory explained to the investigating officer, "It was a sweltering Saturday. I heard someone calling out, so I came down from the second floor and met the gentleman."

"Did you notice anything unusual about him?" the officer inquired, delving into the details of the incident that had culminated in a car crash.

Rory considered the question, his expression thoughtful as he attempted to reconcile the ordinary with the extraordinary tale spun by Jude Bailey. Maintaining a calm demeanor, Rory recounted his perspective to the police officer. "No, he seemed genuinely interested in the building,"

Rory said, recalling Jude Bailey's initial enthusiasm. "He wanted to see the upper floors, so I handed him a set of keys and directed him to the elevator. It slipped my mind to mention that the indicator light was malfunctioning, but I figured it was a minor issue. The elevator would still stop at the floor he selected."

The officer nodded, scribbling notes. "And what happened after that?"

Rory continued, "I didn't accompany him. Most visitors prefer exploring on their own, and I had others to attend to. But he was gone for a considerable time—"

The officer interjected, "How long, exactly?"

Rory pondered, "Perhaps half an hour, maybe a bit more. Time got away from me. When he finally returned, he was standing by the mailboxes. I approached him, tapped his shoulder, and asked about his impression. That's when he screamed, shoved me aside, and bolted out the door, still clutching the keys."

"Did you try to stop him?" the officer probed.

"I attempted to," Rory affirmed, "but he was already in his car, speeding down the slope by the time I reached the entrance. I arrived just in time to witness the collision at the intersection."

The officer, satisfied that Rory's involvement ended there, ceased his questioning, recognizing that the accident was beyond the manager's responsibility.

In the vehicle that collided with Jude Bailey's, there were two familiar faces: Steve Bond, the renowned private detective, and his wife, who had once startled a notorious war criminal into thinking he'd seen a specter. The couple, having built a comfortable life together, were considering a unit in the building and had set out to view it that day.

As they neared the building, Jude Bailey's car hurtled towards them with reckless abandon. Steve Bond's reflexes were sharp; he honked, swerved, and braked, but the impact was inevitable. Fortunately, their skillful maneuvering minimized injury, and they emerged unscathed.

Seeing Jude Bailey unconscious, Steve Bond acted swiftly. He summoned the authorities and an ambulance, ensuring Jude Bailey received medical attention.

Later, at the police station, Steve Bond recounted the incident, corroborating Rory's account that Jude Bailey's erratic behavior led to the crash. Yet, Jude Bailey's tale of a surreal experience in the building added a layer of mystery to the case, one that defied easy explanation. The juxtaposition of reality and the inexplicable left both the police and those involved pondering the strange events that had unfolded.

Chapter 2

Strange Events Reoccur

Steve Bond and I ran into each other by chance, and in the course of our conversation, he casually brought up an intriguing incident involving a man named Jude Bailey, someone I hadn't heard of before. As we talked, I mused aloud, "Some people simply can't handle confined spaces. The claustrophobia of an elevator can trigger inexplicable fear and vivid imaginings."

Steve Bond nodded, "That's what I thought too. This guy must be somewhat high-strung. Yet, there's something about his account that feels oddly tangible."

I added, "There are individuals who blur the line between fantasy and reality. We see it often enough—it's a profound psychological issue."

Steve Bond chuckled, "You should consider psychology as a career. Meanwhile, I'm the real victim here. My car, fresh from Italy, custom-designed and handmade, got wrecked. It's impossible to fix it locally, so I'll be car-less for months!"

I laughed, patting his shoulder, "You're becoming quite the high roller!"

With a grin, Steve Bond replied, "What can I say? People are willing to pay top dollar for my detective skills."

Our conversation meandered to other topics until I asked, "So, did you end up buying the house?"

He shook his head, "I was tempted, but my wife felt the accident was a bad omen, so we decided against it."

"Did you even bother going up to check it out?" I queried.

"Not at all," Steve Bond admitted with a wry smile.

I teased, "If you had, who knows? You might have had an adventure like Mr. Bailey!"

Steve Bond's eyes lit up with sudden excitement, "Let's go see it ourselves! What do you say? I have time, and you could use a diversion."

I hesitated, "Is it really worth it?"

He persisted, "Come on, what's the harm? The building's quite impressive, after all."

The tale of Mr. Bailey's bizarre experience piqued my curiosity, and although I was convinced it was merely a hallucination, the allure of the unknown beckoned. With nothing pressing on my agenda, I agreed to accompany Steve Bond to the building, ready to explore whatever mysteries it might hold.

The road leading to the building's entrance was indeed steep, offering a panoramic view of the towering structure as we approached. The setting sun cast long shadows, and the building, with its imposing height of over 30 floors, loomed majestically in the twilight.

We parked at the entrance and stepped out, joining Steve Bond as we entered the illuminated lobby. The building was still unoccupied, and our footsteps echoed as we crossed the polished floor. Steve Bond called out into the quiet, "Uncle Rory, Uncle Rory!"

Soon enough, Rory descended the staircase, his presence exuding an air of peculiarity. His small eyes seemed to imbue him with an enigmatic quality that was hard to pinpoint.

"Mr. Bond!" Rory greeted warmly, clearly familiar with Steve.

Steve Bond got straight to the point, "I planned to tour the units last time, but the accident cut that short. Have any of the high-rise units been sold since then?"

Rory's expression clouded with confusion. "Strangely, no. Not a single unit has been sold!"

Both Steve Bond and I were taken aback. The building's prime location and architecture should have made it a hot commodity, sold out long before its completion.

"How is that possible?" Steve Bond probed further.

Rory could only shrug. "I can't explain it. Plenty of people come to look, but none commit to buying."

I chuckled, "The owner must be feeling rather unlucky."

Rory, still smiling, replied, "Our boss isn't concerned. He's wealthier than he can manage. Most developers start selling based on blueprints, but he insisted on waiting until completion. Now, not even a single floor is sold. Had he started earlier, it might have been a different story."

Determined, Steve Bond requested, "Could you give me the key to the upper floors? I'd like to have a look."

Rory obliged, "It's getting dark. Take this flashlight," he said, handing over a flashlight along with two keys, both for units on the 23nd floor.

We entered the elevator, leaving Rory behind. As the doors began to close, I quickly inquired, "Have those elevator lights been fixed?"

The door sealed shut, but not before Rory's voice reached us, "Yes, fixed long ago!"

With a press of the "Twenty-three" button, the elevator hummed to life, smoothly ascending. As we rose, I couldn't help but wonder about the strange allure and mystery surrounding this unsold building. Would we encounter the same uncanny experience as Jude Bailey, or was it merely a figment of his imagination? The elevator's ascent was steady, yet the air crackled with anticipation.

Steve Bond and I might not be prone to neurosis, but as the elevator began its ascent, a shared glance confirmed that we both felt a touch of apprehension. Our minds inevitably drifted to the tale of Jude Bailey, and we exchanged a knowing smile, silently dismissing his experience as an anomaly.

The elevator's small lights flickered in a reassuring sequence, counting up each floor—15, 16, 17, and swiftly on to 23. It arrived with a gentle jolt, and the doors slid open with an almost anticlimactic ease.

We exited, sharing another amused look, silently reaffirming our skepticism about Jude Bailey's so-called ordeal. Steve Bond unlocked the door to the unit, and we stepped inside. Darkness enveloped the space, so Steve Bond flicked on the flashlight. The design was impressive— four spacious bedrooms, a living room that opened to a balcony with a breathtaking view of the city's twinkling lights.

Steve Bond was clearly impressed, inspecting each room methodically. He even paused in the bathroom to wash his hands, casually shaking off the droplets. "I've made up my mind," he announced, satisfaction evident in his voice. "I'm buying it."

"Isn't it odd that no one else has?" I mused. "Could be something off about it."

Steve Bond shrugged, unconcerned. "Off? Not a chance. It's perfect."

I teased him, "Won't it be lonely, living here with just your family?"

He chuckled, "That's the idea. I crave the quiet."

We explored another unit on the same floor, identical save for its orientation. Afterwards, we descended to the lobby where Rory awaited. "Count me in as your first buyer,"

Steve Bond declared, handing back the keys. "People don't know what they're missing."

We headed to the car, my mind already on the drive home. But as Steve Bond reached for the door, he stopped abruptly. "Damn, I left my watch in the bathroom when I washed up."

I laughed, "Must be some watch!"

"It's worth as much as a sports car," he grinned. "Wait here, I'll be right back."

I didn't think twice about staying behind. He'd be back soon enough. I watched him return to the building, collect the flashlight and keys from Rory, and step into the elevator.

I waited in the car, yawning as I recalled the many thrilling adventures I'd had with Steve Bond. This, I feared, was shaping up to be the dullest—I was actually accompanying him to see a new house! I shrugged, trying to make myself more comfortable. Settling back in the car, I relaxed to the tune of "Moon River," losing myself in its soothing melody. When the song ended, I glanced at the time. Four minutes had passed, maybe five, certainly enough for Steve Bond to retrieve his watch and return.

I ejected the tape, peering towards the lobby. The lights still glowed warmly, but Rory was nowhere to be seen. My gaze wandered up the building's silhouette against the night sky, an imposing monolith devoid of light. It seemed to loom ominously, casting long shadows that played tricks on the mind.

For a fleeting moment, the memory of Jude Bailey's unsettling account flitted through my thoughts, but I brushed it aside with a chuckle. Steve Bond had been gone for mere minutes. There was nothing to worry about... right?

I had hoped the cigarette would calm my nerves, but as I watched it burn past the halfway mark, my patience wore thin. I tossed the butt aside, stepped out of the car, and approached the building's glass door. Through it, I could see the elevator, but the usual indicator lights were all dark, leaving me clueless about Steve Bond's whereabouts.

Any elevator should display its current position, yet here I was, staring at a dead panel.

Puzzled and increasingly uneasy, I pushed the door open and called out, "Uncle Rory! Uncle Rory!"

Rory descended from the second floor once more, his expression curious. "Mr. Bond hasn't come down yet?"

"No," I replied, frustration creeping into my voice. "He's been up there too long. And why aren't those elevator lights working?"

Rory cast a glance at the elevator and sighed, "The light's broken again. Happens a lot—quite a nuisance."

I paced the lobby, anxiety mounting with each step. As I finished another cigarette, I turned to Rory, "Is there really only one elevator?"

"Yes," he confirmed, "this building only has one."

"Then where's the service elevator?" I pressed, hoping for another way to reach Steve Bond.

Rory shook his head, "There isn't one. Just the main elevator."

I felt a chill run down my spine. The thought of Steve Bond possibly stuck somewhere in the building, with no way to reach him except through an unreliable elevator, was unsettling. I pondered my next move, my mind racing with scenarios, each more troubling than the last. It seemed as if the building itself was conspiring to keep its secrets hidden, and I was determined to uncover them, to find Steve Bond and ensure his safety.

In many high-end buildings like this one, it's common to have a service or back elevator, so I asked Rory about it. But he shook his head, explaining, "No, maybe that's why it hasn't sold. Many people have asked about additional elevators, and they're put off when there isn't one."

I turned back to the elevator, pressing the button repeatedly while pressing my ear against the door. There was a faint noise, a distant hum that could be the steel cables in motion. The elevator might be moving — ascending or, hopefully, descending as Steve Bond returned.

Yet, after three minutes of expectant waiting, there was still no sign of Steve Bond. I glanced at Rory and noticed his eyes were wide, his face pale and expression oddly tense. My call startled him, and I announced my plan to take the stairs. "If Mr. Bond comes down, make sure he waits for me," I instructed.

Rory seemed bewildered, "Sir, you're going to the 23rd floor?"

Ignoring his question, I sprinted to the staircase and began my ascent, two steps at a time. My training in martial arts gave me the endurance to maintain this pace, though I knew it would be grueling.

At each landing, I checked the elevator's position, using my lighter to illuminate the unlit indicators. But every floor showed the same result—dark, inactive lights.

Breathless by the 20th floor, I was determined to continue. I shouted for Steve Bond, my voice echoing into the silence. Reaching the 23rd floor, I called out again, but the only response was the emptiness of the unoccupied space.

The door to the unit was locked; my banging yielded nothing but echoes. Anxiety clawed at me as I pounded on the elevator doors, suspecting Steve Bond might be trapped within. The chilling stillness was unnerving, and I realized I needed to contact the elevator company for help. I turned to descend.

Running up more than twenty floors in succession felt akin to running ten thousand meters. My legs were heavy and protesting, yet urgency spurred me on. Around the 4th or 5th floor, Rory's voice reached me, his worried call slicing through the air, "Mr. Bond, what's wrong with you?"

Then came Steve Bond's voice — a disturbing, unrecognizable shout followed by the sound of something or someone colliding forcefully with a surface.

Adrenaline surged, and I leapt down the stairs, propelled by fear for my friend, desperate to reach the lobby and uncover what had transpired.

When I reached the lobby, I found Rory propped against the wall near the mailboxes, struggling to regain his footing. I rushed over to help him stand, and as I did, I noticed the elevator had descended and its doors stood open.

"Where is Mr. Bond?" I demanded urgently.

Rory, still catching his breath, pointed outside. Without waiting for him to speak, I turned my gaze to the entrance and saw Steve Bond getting into his car. Even from a distance, his movements were frantic and hurried, as if he were fleeing from a dire threat.

I shouted his name, "Steve Bond!" and sprinted towards the exit. In my haste, I collided with the glass door, the impact leaving me momentarily disoriented.

By the time I managed to push the door open, Steve Bond's car had already roared to life. The vehicle screeched as it peeled away, skidding around the corner and racing down the road without its headlights on.

I chased after him, but he disappeared into the night, leaving me standing in bewilderment. Clearly, something had terrified him deeply—enough to make him forget that I was with him and prompt such a reckless departure.

Unsure of what to do next, I lingered, until Rory emerged, his face marked by the same alarm. Before I could question him, he asked, "What happened to Mr. Bond?"

I echoed his concern, "I was going to ask you the same thing. What happened?"

Rory recounted, "I was waiting here when the elevator opened. As Mr. Bond stepped out, I tried to tell him that you had gone upstairs to find him. But before I could speak, he shoved me aside. I called after him, but he shouted incoherently, pushed me down, and bolted outside. That's when you arrived."

"Did he say anything at all?" I pressed.

Rory shook his head, confirming Steve Bond's silence.

"What did he look like?" I asked, hoping for a clue.

Rory's reaction was unsettling, his eyes wide with fear as he struggled to articulate his thoughts. "It's terrible, just like—just like—" he stammered, but I quickly interjected, "Just like Mr. Bailey last time?"

His rapid nodding sent a chill down my spine. If Steve Bond had experienced something similar to Jude Bailey, it implied that the elevator had taken him on an inexplicable journey, ascending without stopping for an unnaturally long time.

I took a deep breath, trying to steady my nerves. "Rory, have you ever experienced anything unusual with this elevator?"

Rory's expression was one of genuine alarm. "Sir, don't scare me like that. I use this elevator countless times every day!"

Seeing his sincerity, I realized my question was redundant, but I pressed further, "Have you ever encountered anything strange?"

He shook his head emphatically.

I returned to the elevator, determined to see for myself. Rory trailed behind but halted when I motioned for him to stay back. I pressed the button for the 23rd floor. The elevator doors closed, and it swiftly rose, passing the 10th floor in the blink of an eye.

As the numbers climbed past 20, I felt a tension build within me. When the display reached "23," the elevator halted with a familiar jolt, and the doors opened onto a quiet, empty hallway—nothing out of the ordinary.

I retraced my steps, ascending to the top floor and descending agian, returning to the lobby, where Rory awaited with a look of profound curiosity. "Sir, is everything okay?" he asked.

I didn't answer immediately, my mind awash with questions. The elevator had functioned perfectly for me—no anomalies, no inexplicable stops.

Yet both Jude Bailey and Steve Bond had experienced something unsettling. Why? What was different?

As I pondered, I recalled the small lights. "Were the elevator's lights working when I went up?" I asked Rory.

He confirmed, "Yes, they were."

I nodded, a sense of unease lingering as I exited the building. The area was remote, and it took a while before I could flag down a streetcar. As I waited, the throbbing on my forehead reminded me of my earlier collision with the glass door.

Once aboard, I directed the driver to Steve Bond's address, arriving ten minutes later. I pressed the doorbell, one hand still cradling my swollen brow.

Mrs. Bond greeted me warmly, her cheer contrasting sharply with my concern. "You are so welcome, long time no see!" she exclaimed.

Her words sank my heart. Steve Bond hadn't returned yet.

"Where is Steve Bond?" I asked urgently.

Mrs. Bond smiled, "Please come in and sit down. He's a man of uncertain times. Who knows when he'll be home!"

Standing at the threshold, I hesitated, my demeanor prompting her to study me more closely. "Just now, I was with him," I explained.

Her surprise grew. "We went to that building to look at houses," I continued. "You know, the one where that reckless guy hit your car last time."

Recognition flashed in her eyes. "Of course I remember. What happened to him?"

"I wish I knew," I replied grimly. "Something spooked him. He left in such a hurry. I'm going to find him."

As I turned to leave, Mrs. Bond called after me, "What happened?"

I was already at the stairs, urgency driving me. "I don't have time to explain. He drove down that slope faster than the guy who hit your car!"

With that, I dashed out, my mind racing as I headed to find my friend and uncover the mystery that had ensnared him.

Mrs. Bond's anxious cries echoed in my mind as I dashed down the stairs, my heart pounding with urgency. "Contact me anytime!" I shouted back at her, hoping to reassure her as I reached the street and hailed another streetcar.

Throughout the night, I directed the driver through the city, tracing paths between the building and Steve Bond's home, hoping to catch a glimpse of his car. Every time I spotted a phone booth, I called Mrs. Bond, only to hear her increasingly tearful voice, "No, he's not back yet."

The streetcar driver eyed me with a mix of concern and confusion, probably wondering about my relentless pursuit and frequent calls to the police. Each time I inquired about accidents, they'd list off incidents, none involving Steve Bond. Part of me irrationally hoped to find his car at least damaged on the roadside, but no such luck.

As dawn broke, the driver, understandably exhausted, informed me he needed to rest. I thanked him, paid, and stepped into the early morning light, feeling a weight of hopelessness. Where could Steve Bond have gone? The mystery of the elevator seemed trivial compared to his disappearance.

I called Mrs. Bond one last time at eight in the morning, urging her to report Steve Bond's disappearance to the police. Despite my fatigue, I returned to her house, supporting her as we went to the station. There, familiar faces greeted me, but I was too preoccupied to exchange pleasantries.

After filing the report, a police officer approached me with news: "There's a car floating near the seashore. We're in the process of retrieving it. The license plate number is—" He recited the number, and I felt my heart skip a beat. Mrs. Bond gasped, then crumpled to the floor in a faint.

Chaos ensued as she was rushed to the hospital, and I hurried to the beach. A crowd had gathered, drawn by the spectacle of a salvage operation. A police boat and a barge with a crane were extracting a waterlogged vehicle from the sea, streams of saltwater cascading from its frame.

As I watched, dread gripped me. Had Steve Bond, in his panic, driven off the road and plunged into the sea? The possibility was devastating.

Once the car was secured on deck, the police examined it. To everyone's astonishment, the doors were locked, and no one was inside. It seemed as though Steve Bond had parked in a garage, locked up, and simply left. Yet, the car had been submerged.

The bizarre circumstances left me perplexed, but a glimmer of hope arose—Steve Bond hadn't been in the car when it sank. It stood to reason that he couldn't have left the vehicle and secured it underwater.

The relief was palpable, though questions remained. Where was Steve Bond now, and what had driven him to such desperate actions? The mystery deepened, but knowing he wasn't trapped in the car provided a small comfort amidst the uncertainty.

Chapter 3

The Disappearance

The police officer turned to his men and instructed them to notify Mrs. Bond at the hospital that Mr. Bond could not have been in the car when it plunged into the sea. I walked forward to examine the vehicle.

This was the car Steve Bond had driven with me to the building. It was now filled with water, and the keys were conspicuously absent.

I couldn't fathom how the car had ended up in the sea, but that wasn't my primary concern. What I truly cared about was Steve Bond's whereabouts.

Three days later, this question dominated the headlines and became a matter of public interest. Steve Bond had not been seen since he drove down that slope.

The police were fully engaged in the search. Steve Bond, a successful detective with a prominent agency and a team of highly capable assistants, was missing. With so many people looking for him, it was as if even a needle in a haystack could be found, yet Steve Bond remained elusive.

The discovery of his valuable watch in the bathroom on the 23rd floor only deepened the enigma. He had returned to retrieve it, yet left it behind, suggesting he never actually entered the unit. This detail ruled out the possibility that he had simply forgotten it after entering.

Rory was cleared of suspicion since I had witnessed Steve Bond's frantic departure. Ironically, I found myself under scrutiny. However, Mrs. Bond, despite her heartbreak and anxiety, staunchly defended the friendship between Steve Bond and me, asserting that I would never harm him.

After five chaotic days, I finally had a moment to reflect alone, and I recalled Jude Bailey's experience.

When I had waited for Steve Bond and saw him rush out of the building in a panic, Jude Bailey's experience had crossed my mind. However, during the subsequent investigation, I never shared these thoughts with anyone.

The police were aware of Jude Bailey's experience after the car accident, so there was no need for me to mention it.

Besides, such an absurd story couldn't serve as the basis for a formal investigation.

After the incident, I had ridden that very elevator multiple times, hoping to encounter something out of the ordinary. Yet, each journey was uneventful, the machinery functioning smoothly, as if mocking the notion of anything supernatural.

However, the sheer oddity of Steve Bond's disappearance gnawed at me. It felt as though we were dealing with forces beyond our understanding, elements that defied logic and reason.

Determined to explore every possibility, I resolved to visit Jude Bailey. Perhaps his firsthand account could shed light on what Steve Bond might have experienced. It was a long shot, but given the circumstances, I couldn't afford to dismiss any potential lead.

With renewed resolve, I set out to find Jude Bailey, hoping his insights might unravel the mystery and bring Steve Bond back safely.

* * *

I decided to visit Jude Bailey at his workplace, a large commercial organization with strict policies about private meetings during work hours. Luckily, I leveraged my own import-export business as a pretext, arranging a meeting under the guise of discussing potential business collaborations.

When Jude Bailey arrived, he appeared to be a typical professional: around 40 years old, well-educated, and composed. However, the fresh scars on his cheeks—remnants of the accident with Steve Bond—hinted at more turbulent times beneath his calm exterior.

Initially, we discussed business matters, and he quickly informed me that his organization couldn't assist with my inquiries. I then shifted the conversation to a more personal topic. "Mr. Bailey, I heard you had a rather unsettling experience in an elevator recently?"

His demeanor changed abruptly; he stood up, visibly distressed. It seemed his professional decorum was the only thing preventing an outburst. With a strained expression, he said, "Mr. Morris, I think it's time for you to leave."

Sensing an opportunity, I calmly mentioned, "Do you recall Mr. Bond, the owner of the car you collided with?"

This caught him off guard. "Yes, he's gone missing!" The news had indeed made waves, and Jude Bailey was clearly aware of it.

Continuing, I said, "You know the circumstances surrounding his disappearance? I was with him just before it happened. There's something I haven't shared with anyone—because it sounds unbelievable. It took Mr. Bond at least fifteen minutes from entering to exiting the elevator."

Jude Bailey's pallor deepened, his fear palpable. "More than fifteen minutes... really more than," he murmured, almost to himself.

I pressed on, "What exactly happened? Was the elevator continuously ascending during all that time?"

His terror was unmistakable, his face contorting, eyes wide with a haunted look. His lips quivered as he struggled to speak. Despite my reluctance to push him further, I needed answers. After a prolonged silence, he confirmed, "Yes, the elevator kept rising, rising all the time."

I approached him, hoping to steady his nerves. "Mr. Bailey," I said gently, "we're both rational, educated adults. Does this seem possible? An elevator rising several thousand feet within nearly 20 minutes?"

Jude Bailey's response was a vacant whisper, "I don't know, I don't know."

His fear seemed genuine, and I realized that whatever he had experienced had left a profound mark. His story resonated with the bizarre circumstances of Steve Bond's disappearance. Although I had more questions, it was clear I needed to tread carefully, respecting the trauma he had endured while seeking the truth.

I pressed further, "So, Mr. Bailey, what happened after the elevator finally stopped?"

To my surprise, Jude Bailey seemed to regain his composure almost immediately. "Nothing happened," he replied, a bit too quickly. Realizing his response might seem dismissive, he added, "I've already explained everything to many people in the hospital, and Mr. Bond knew about it too. I really don't want to discuss it anymore."

I recalled Steve Bond's relay of what happened after the elevator stopped—how he found himself in a residential unit, gazing from a balcony into a void of gray, devoid of sky or ground. I trusted Steve Bond's recounting, but Jude Bailey's sudden calmness and evasive answers made me suspect he was withholding information about what truly transpired after the elevator stopped.

Sensing his reluctance, I tried to approach delicately. "Could you possibly share your experience with me again? Knowing what happened could help me understand what Steve Bond went through."

But Jude Bailey was firm. "I'm sorry, I'm busy, and we've discussed your business already," he replied, signaling the end of our conversation.

I persisted, "Then perhaps we could talk about it sometime outside of work? Steve Bond is my best friend, and I need to know what happened to him."

Jude Bailey forced a smile, his tone dismissive. "The doctors say it was just a mental state caused by stress. I agree with them. Mr. Bond's disappearance is unrelated. Please don't contact me about this again."

It was clear he was evading, possibly concealing something significant. However, without further evidence, I couldn't push him more at that moment. Reluctantly, I watched him leave the room, and shortly after, I exited the building myself.

Determined not to give up, I decided to wait in my car in the parking lot until the end of the workday. As employees trickled out, I spotted Jude Bailey among them. He appeared unremarkable, blending in with the crowd, seemingly unaware of my watchful eyes.

I tailed him discreetly as he left the parking lot. Without a clear plan, I hoped that understanding Jude Bailey's true experience might lead to a breakthrough in finding Steve Bond.

Navigating through the congested traffic, I kept a careful distance. Eventually, the roads cleared, and Jude Bailey stopped at a bakery. After picking up a paper box, he continued his journey.

It seemed like a normal day in a normal neighborhood when Jude Bailey parked his car on a side street and entered a modest three-story house. I observed him from a distance, noting how ordinary everything appeared. Despite his earlier evasiveness, there was no hint of anything unusual or suspicious in his demeanor.

Nonetheless, driven by the urgency of finding Steve Bond, I decided to approach Jude Bailey again, though I knew it might not be well-received. After deliberating in my car, I finally walked up to the third floor of the building, where a door with a copper plate engraved "Bailey's House" marked his home.

I rang the doorbell, and Jude Bailey answered, his expression darkening upon seeing me. "Mr. Morris, what do you mean by this?" he demanded.

Acknowledging my intrusion, I pleaded, "Mr. Bailey, I'm sorry for bothering you, but I really need your help to find Steve Bond."

His patience worn thin, he replied, "I can't help you. I warn you, don't bother me again."

From inside, a woman's voice called out, asking who was at the door. "I don't know, just a nuisance," Jude Bailey responded, before slamming the door shut.

In that brief moment, I considered forcing my way in, but I restrained myself and stood there briefly before descending the stairs.

The following morning, I was startled awake by a visit from a police officer. His demeanor was stern as he informed me, "We've received a complaint that you're harassing Mr. Bailey."

Caught off guard, I attempted to explain, "I was only trying to ask him some questions to find clues about the missing Steve—"

However, the officer cut me off, "Mr. Bailey has filed a complaint with a doctor's certificate. He's suffering from severe neurasthenia, and any harassment could worsen his condition. You need to cease all contact with him."

I was momentarily speechless, then replied with a touch of sarcasm, "Bailey's nerves have been troubled for a while, not because of me. Surely you're aware of his elevator story in that building?"

The officer shrugged, "That's his concern. Bottom line, he doesn't want to be bothered."

Realizing I had no choice but to comply, I nodded, feeling the weight of the situation. Despite my frustration, I understood that I needed to respect Jude Bailey's wishes, even if it meant losing a potential lead. My next steps would require a different approach, and I had to find another way to uncover the truth about Steve Bond's disappearance.

I agreed to the officer's request, albeit reluctantly. "Okay, but please relay to Colonel Jack that I believe Jude Bailey is harboring a secret, one that could be crucial to understanding Steve Bond's disappearance."

Colonel Jack, known for handling particularly unusual cases, was in charge of the investigation. Although we were well-acquainted, our relationship was characterized by a mutual stubbornness and frequent disagreements. We tended to avoid each other unless necessary, as our encounters often ended in arguments rather than cooperation.

My mention of Colonel Jack caught the officer's attention. "Before coming here, the colonel had a message for you," he said.

I raised an eyebrow, curious about Jack's message.

"The colonel said he appreciates the efforts you and Mr. Bond's team are making, but he believes they won't lead to finding Mr. Bond if the police haven't succeeded."

I chuckled at the message, recognizing the familiar tone of our disagreements. Without hesitation, I replied, "Please thank the colonel for his advice, but let him know that if we can't find Mr. Bond, neither can the police."

The officer departed, leaving me to contemplate my next steps. Shortly afterward, I headed to Steve Bond's detective agency, which I had been visiting daily since his disappearance. In his absence, I had unofficially taken charge, focusing the agency's resources solely on locating him.

Upon arrival, two of the agency's most dedicated staff members reported in. They were part of a team I had stationed to keep watch over Mrs. Bond around the clock. My reasoning was simple: if Steve Bond's disappearance was linked to a case involving a criminal organization, Mrs. Bond could also be at risk. By watching her, we might uncover new leads.

However, each report from the team was discouraging. Mrs. Bond remained undisturbed, aside from visits from concerned friends and family. While she was undoubtedly the most grief-stricken, there was no sign of the trouble I hoped might provide us with leads.

Acknowledging Mrs. Bond's sorrow, I found myself at a loss for words of comfort. My sole focus remained on finding Steve Bond, provided he was still alive.

The circumstances of his disappearance were so strange, especially the detail of his car being found locked at sea. My suspicion was that he encountered foul play and that someone subsequently locked the vehicle before disposing of it in the ocean.

The pivotal question remained: what exactly had happened to Steve Bond? And who could be behind such a calculated act? Finding answers required following every possible lead, no matter how tenuous, and maintaining hope that something might eventually break the case wide open.

Colonel Jack's message was clear: he believed our efforts were futile. Yet, I was convinced that our approach differed significantly from that of the police. While they might not consider certain avenues worth pursuing, we were willing to explore every possibility.

After instructing my staff members to continue safeguarding Mrs. Bond, another team member handed me a sizeable stack of documents. "We managed to obtain the original design drawings of the building," he stated. "All the information is here."

As I began poring over the architectural plans, I couldn't help but wonder if understanding this building might somehow lead us to Steve Bond. At first glance, the design appeared typical, with one notable exception: the building had only one elevator.

In the midst of the documents, a small piece of paper caught my attention. It contained a single line that left me momentarily stunned: " The original design called for three elevators, but according to the owner's opinion, only one will be installed."

The note, photocopied and bearing an indecipherable signature, piqued my curiosity. I quickly scanned the rest of the documents, trying to piece together the implications of this decision.

The note suggested that the "owner" of the building had made the unusual decision to limit it to a single elevator. Typically, a real estate project follows a standard process: acquiring land, forming a development company, designing the building, contracting construction, and eventually selling units.

Originally, the design included three elevators—two in the lobby and one at the back, which is standard. However, the owner had insisted on a solitary elevator for the entire structure, a choice any architect would find unusual. Yet, they complied, resulting in a redesign.

The building's failure to sell units might have been due to this odd elevator setup, leading to financial losses for the owner. But the larger question remained: why would the owner insist on such a peculiar design?

Common sense couldn't explain this decision. There must have been a specific reason, possibly linked to the strange occurrences reported by Jude Bailey in the elevator. I suspected that Steve Bond, retrieving his watch alone, had experienced something similar, prompting his sudden, inexplicable departure.

The discovery of this note was crucial. It suggested a deeper mystery surrounding the building's design and the elevator's singular existence. Whatever the reason, it seemed intertwined with the bizarre events and Steve Bond's disappearance. I needed to dig deeper, possibly uncovering the motivations behind the owner's unconventional demand and how it might connect to the ongoing mystery.

After considering all this, I looked at the designer's name in the corner of the drawing. It read "Edward Clark Architects Office" along with its phone number and address.

I pressed the intercom button and invited the two staff members in. "Go check as soon as possible who owns this building. I'm heading out now, but I'll call you back!"

The staff members exchanged disapproving glances. One of them moved his lips but remained silent, while the other spoke up, "Mr. Morris, what does the owner have to do with Mr. Bond's disappearance?"

I waved my hand, interrupting him. "No direct connection, right?"

They nodded, clearly eager for an explanation.

I paused, unsure how to articulate my thoughts, but finally said, "Mr. Bond's disappearance is not ordinary. There must be mysterious and unknowable factors involved. We have to pursue every clue."

I stood up, patted them on the shoulders, and continued, "Do as I say. I hope to get results the first time I call back."

As I walked towards the door, I added, "You don't need to contact Edward Clark Architects Office. I'll go see the architect now. If he knows who the owner is, that would be best."

I walked out, sensing their skepticism despite their agreement.

Navigating through the crowded streets, I entered a building, squeezed into and out of an elevator, pushed open the door to Edward Clark Architects Office, and walked in.

The architectural firm was sizable and bustling with staff. I explained my purpose to one of them, who then led me to a female secretary.

The secretary, wearing thick glasses and appearing thin and dry, glanced up briefly before resuming her novel. "What's the matter?"

"I'd like to see architect Edward Clark," I stated.

"Do you have an appointment?" she asked without looking up.

I admitted that I didn't, realizing she'd missed my head shake since she was engrossed in her book. "No," I added verbally.

With a sigh, she set aside her novel and retrieved a notebook. "Name?" she inquired, jotting down my response, "Ash Morris," on a line.

"Why are you seeking a meeting?" she continued, still not making eye contact.

"It's complicated," I replied, aware that my answer lacked the specificity that might expedite my request. "It can't be explained in one or two sentences."

"Okay," she murmured nonchalantly, scribbling "unknown" beside my name, a detail that struck me as both amusing and frustrating.

"Phone?" she asked next, maintaining her dispassionate demeanor.

Feeling a bit exasperated, I reiterated my urgency. "Miss, I really need to speak with Mr. Clark. It's important."

The secretary finally glanced up, her expression flat. "Mr. Clark is very busy. Appointments are necessary, and your slot is at 10 a.m. the day after tomorrow. You'll have 20 minutes. If you're late, it's your loss."

Realizing I was caught in bureaucracy, I couldn't help but chuckle at the absurdity of it all. "He's just an architect, not an emperor," I quipped, attempting to lighten the mood.

Her icy response echoed her earlier sentiment. "That's the rule here."

A few employees nearby had taken notice of our exchange, and I spread my hands in resignation. "Alright, but this is urgent. I need to ask him something very important."

Unmoved, she insisted, "Come early the day after tomorrow."

Deciding to take matters into my own hands, I strode past her toward the door marked "Architect Edward Clark." Her cry of protest followed me, but I was undeterred.

In the office, I faced a middle-aged man with gray hair, busy reviewing documents. His surprise at my entrance was evident, but I quickly apologized. "I'm sorry, Mr. Clark, but I have something important to discuss."

To my relief, he smiled and invited me in, dismissing the secretary's concerns. "Miss Cox, please close the door. This gentleman says he has urgent business."

After she reluctantly complied, I introduced myself and launched into the purpose of my visit. "Mr. Clark, I understand you've designed many buildings, but one stands out—a building originally meant to have three elevators, but reduced to one at the owner's insistence."

Edward Clark nodded, recalling the project. "Yes, I remember. It's been a while since it was completed, but it hasn't sold."

I confirmed his memory, noting the building's vacant status. "Exactly. It remains empty."

"I warned the owner," Edward Clark remarked, shaking his head. "Changing the design wouldn't affect the structure, but it would make the building undesirable. He wouldn't listen."

Intrigued, I pressed on. "Do you remember who this owner is?"

Chen thought for a moment, appearing to sift through his memories. "I might have some old records. Let me check."

As he searched, I felt hopeful. If he could recall the owner, it might provide a crucial link to unraveling the mystery of Steve Bond's disappearance.

Chapter 4

Elderly in Seclusion

I pressed again, delving deeper into the enigma of the building's unconventional design. "The owner's insistence on altering the design—was there a particular reason behind it?"

Edward Clark, the architect, responded with a slight shake of his head, a gesture that spoke volumes of unspoken mysteries. "None that he shared with me, at least. Perhaps he had his motives, but they remained his own."

He paused, the weight of unsold floors and empty corridors heavy in the air. "Why the interest in this building? If its market failure is due to the elevator issue, reversing that decision would be no simple task."

I offered a reassuring smile, a mask for my ulterior motives. "I'm not here on behalf of the owner. My curiosity is piqued solely by the identity of this elusive owner."

For a moment, the architect seemed taken aback, caught in a moment of reflection. He hesitated, and I seized the pause.

"Is it a matter of confidentiality?" I asked, probing further. "A business secret, perhaps, that prevents you from revealing his identity?"

I braced myself for the expected denial, ready to lay bare the tangled web involving Jude Bailey and Steve Bond. Surely such intrigue would capture his interest and loosen his tongue.

Yet, in this complex tapestry of assumptions, I found myself misguided. Edward Clark's expression turned pensive. "Reflecting on it now, it strikes me as peculiar. Throughout our dealings, I never learned his full name. He was simply Mr. Darcy—a shadowy figure who visited me frequently, his residence a mystery."

His revelation left me momentarily speechless. "Do you recall what he looked like?"

A nod from Edward Clark. "Indeed. An emaciated old man, yet exuding an air of wealth—enough to indulge his whims with impunity."

I rose, extending my hand in gratitude. "Thank you for your time, Mr. Clark."

As I exited, the secretary's glare followed me, a silent rebuke for my breach of protocol. I returned her look with a playful smirk, then signaled to a staff member for the use of their phone.

I dialed Steve Bond's office, anticipation coursing through me. "Have you discovered the owner's name and whereabouts?"

The reply came swiftly, "We traced the land ownership to a company registration. The title belongs to a Max Darcy."

"Perfect. And this Darcy — his surname matches." I confirmed.

"Indeed, Max Darcy. The address is a suburban locale, Highway 7, Section 983, at a place known as 'Fludent Garden'—likely a villa."

"Excellent," I said, the pieces aligning in my mind. "I'm heading to see Mr. Darcy now."

I put down the phone, leaving the architect's office with a sense of purpose and a mind brimming with possibilities.

The prospect of meeting the enigmatic owner who had insisted on the peculiar elevator design filled me with anticipation. Surely, this encounter would shed light on the mystery that had been shrouding Steve Bond's disappearance.

With determination fueling my drive, I headed straight for the suburbs. Highway No. 7, a sinewy branch road etched into the sprawling landscape, wound its way toward an ethereal mountain shrouded in mist, where only a smattering of houses dared to cling to its slopes. As my car ascended, the sun intermittently pierced the cloud cover, casting radiant beams that danced across the terrain, turning the mundane into the magnificent.

After twenty minutes of navigating the serpentine mountain road, the landscape transformed. A row of brick walls, adorned with green-glazed tile eaves, emerged from the mist. Soon after, I encountered the imposing main gate of Fludent Garden, its name etched boldly into the stone. The estate sprawled across the entire valley, its walls stretching endlessly, concealing whatever lay within from prying eyes.

I halted the car, stepping into the serene yet mysterious embrace of the mountain. Fludent Garden presented itself as a fortress of antiquity, its bronze gate exuding a sense of permanence and tradition, hinting at the character of the owner—a man, perhaps, as immovable as the mountains themselves.

Pausing to gather my thoughts, I scoured for a doorbell, but none graced this grand entrance. Instead, a hefty copper ring hung on the door, its purpose clear. With a sense of old-world ritual, I lifted it and let it fall against the bronze with a resounding clang that echoed through the quiet mountain air.

The silence that followed was profound, but after a brief wait, a "click" disrupted the stillness. A small square aperture opened in the door, revealing a timeworn face that peered at me with curiosity.

"I seek Mr. Max Darcy," I announced, meeting the guardian's gaze.

The face regarded me with skepticism, scrutinizing my features before responding. "And your business?"

Prepared for this inquiry, I replied, "I am a construction businessman interested in purchasing the building he developed. My name is Ash Morris."

The face lingered a moment longer, then nodded. "Please wait here," it instructed before the aperture closed with a muted thud.

Resigned to my wait, I paced the cobbled path, tracing the history of footsteps long faded. Time crept forward, the minutes stretching into twenty, and still, the door remained unyielding. Impatience gnawed at me, compelling me back to the gate. Just as my hand reached for the copper ring, the door swung open with a creak, inviting me into the unknown.

As the door creaked open, the same man stood there— a servant by appearance, clad in a short grey cloth coat that spoke of a life spent attending to others' needs. "Please, come in. The master awaits you in the living room," he said, his voice as steady as the mountain air.

I nodded, stepping into a world that seemed meticulously curated yet naturally serene. The garden before me was a testament to the art of eastern courtyard design. Twisting corridors formed by ancient wisterias led the way, with trees, vibrant flowers, and gravel paths guiding my journey. Even a few cranes graced the scene, adding to the timeless elegance.

Navigating the garden felt like traversing a labyrinth of nature's artistry. The silence of the servant behind me was palpable, his presence a silent guide through this verdant maze. I refrained from conversation, respecting the tranquility of the moment.

The house emerged slowly from behind the foliage, an architectural relic of genuine antiquity that seemed to transport me to an era long past. Unlike the faux historical facades designed for tourists, this was a residence steeped in authenticity and history. Its vast hall exuded a sense of comfort and ease, inviting relaxation.

I was ushered to a marble chair adorned with natural landscape patterns, a masterpiece in its own right. The servant returned with a cup of green tea, its steam curling into the air like an ethereal offering. "Please wait a moment; the master will join you shortly," he said before retreating.

The silence enveloped me, broken only by the soft rustle of bamboo leaves swaying in a gentle breeze. It was a symphony of nature, a perfect accompaniment to the serene surroundings. I found solace in the art and literature that adorned the walls, each piece a story waiting to be told.

Footsteps echoed through the hall, drawing my attention to the source. An old man entered—medium build, ruddy complexion, vitality evident despite the cane he leaned on. His presence was commanding, yet his gaze was kind.

As I regarded him, I mused that Max Darcy would have been at home in the flowing robes of antiquity, a figure from a bygone era. Even in his modern suit, he exuded an air of distinction, a testament to his character.

He introduced himself with a nod, "I am Max Darcy."

I returned his greeting with a respectful bow, marveling at how different he was from the description given by Edward Clark. Clearly, the architect's portrayal had been lacking.

"Mr. Darcy, I apologize for the intrusion. Your abode is truly a sanctuary," I remarked, genuinely awed by the tranquil beauty of his home—a stark contrast to the cacophony of urban life.

Max Darcy's smile was serene as he gestured for me to sit. The servant reappeared, serving tea with practiced grace.

We exchanged pleasantries at first, our conversation meandering like the garden paths. Then, Max Darcy steered it toward the matter at hand. "Mr. Morris, I hear you're interested in my building?"

I nodded eagerly. "Indeed, its location is prime. It's surprising that not a single unit has been sold."

His response was a nonchalant shrug, a man unfazed by what others might see as failure. "My lifestyle is unaffected. If it remains unsold, so be it. An empty building is not a burden to me."

Hearing Mr. Darcy's indifferent remark left me momentarily stunned. I realized that if I didn't cut through the pleasantries and get to the heart of the matter swiftly, my journey here would amount to nothing. Leaning forward, I decided to lay my cards on the table. "Mr. Darcy, before coming to see you, I had a conversation with the designer of your building, Mr. Clark."

Max Darcy nodded, his expression unchanged. "Yes, I remember Mr. Clark."

I met his gaze, determined to gauge his reaction. "The original plans for this building included three elevators. But it was at your insistence that the design was altered to just one."

I paused, scrutinizing his demeanor for any sign of unease or revelation, but Mr. Darcy remained as placid as a mountain lake, unfazed by the significance of the change.

Pressing on, I asked directly, "Mr. Darcy, was there a particular reason for altering the original design?"

His response was as unexpected as it was disarming. "I don't care for modern contraptions—" He gestured around us, encompassing the timeless elegance of his surroundings. "Elevators trap people in metal boxes, hoisting them skyward. Why not walk? We have legs for a reason."

His reasoning, while peculiar, was not without its own logic given his lifestyle and environment. It left me momentarily at a loss for words. In his world, his philosophy made perfect sense.

Yet, despite his explanation, I couldn't shake the feeling that there was more to this story, something elusive and enigmatic lurking beneath the surface.

I managed a smile, though my mind raced. "Mr. Darcy, your building stands over twenty stories tall. Surely, you don't expect residents to climb all those flights of stairs."

Max Darcy chuckled softly. "The ancients dwelt on mountainsides, after all. They scaled heights daily without complaint. And besides, there's still an elevator."

I pushed further. "Have you visited the building since it was completed?"

He nodded. "Once, only once. The city holds no allure for me—I prefer my solitude."

I seized the thread of contradiction in his story. "Yet, you met with architect Edward Clark multiple times. That seems—"

It seemed, I was about to say, at odds with his professed disdain for urban life. If he truly detested the city's modernity, why even conceive of such a project?

But before I could voice my thought, Max Darcy's gaze met mine, filled with a knowing that bordered on the cryptic. It was as if he understood the contradiction perfectly, and perhaps, there lay the key to the mystery I sought to unravel.

The contradiction gnawed at me. If Max Darcy had been invested enough to commission a building and visit the architect multiple times, it seemed implausible that he would only visit the completed structure once simply because he disliked the city. Yet, I chose not to voice this skepticism aloud, for just as I was about to, I caught a fleeting flicker of annoyance in his eyes—a glimpse of vulnerability as if I had brushed too close to a concealed truth.

He maintained his calm composure, "The building is complete, and I have someone managing it. There's no need for me to visit again. Mr. Morris, if you're interested, you could purchase it."

I scrutinized him, deciding to reveal more. "Mr. Darcy, to be honest, I've visited your building numerous times. While I haven't personally encountered anything unusual, two others have had strange experiences in the elevator. One of them—my good friend—has been missing for several days because of it."

Max Darcy's face twisted into a strange expression, a mix of curiosity and disbelief. "Strange? What kind of strange occurrences?"

"Evidently, after entering the elevator, it continued ascending to an unknown place," I explained.

Momentarily taken aback, Max Darcy laughed dismissively, "I can't fathom what you're suggesting. Elevators rise; that's their purpose."

I attempted to clarify, "Yes, but it ascends for much longer than expected. What I mean is—"

Yet, words failed me, the peculiarity of the situation challenging to articulate. "Mr. Darcy, surely you've used an elevator before?"

Anticipating affirmation, I was ready to delve further, but instead, Max Darcy shook his head. "I've never taken an elevator."

I was at a loss. In this day and age, it seemed improbable for anyone to have avoided using an elevator. "But you said you've visited your building and met with the architect—"

"Yes," he interjected, "but I always took the stairs."

His subsequent words unraveled the mystery somewhat. "I avoid elevators because they frighten me. Being enclosed in a metal box, uncertain of where it might take you—it's unnerving."

I could only muster a wry smile. For someone who had never experienced the confines of an elevator, explaining the strange occurrences experienced by Jude Bailey and others was futile. It seemed my visit had yielded little.

With a sigh, I stood. "I apologize for intruding on your peaceful life. I should be going."

Max Darcy's eyes lingered on me. "Before you go, you mentioned a missing friend. What happened?"

I gave a brief account, "I'm unsure what he saw in the elevator. He went up alone, and when he didn't return, I waited. Eventually, he rushed out, drove away, and vanished."

I relayed the story more out of obligation than expectation, noting Max Darcy's polite yet indifferent demeanor.

His response was a simple, understanding "Oh," before rising to call for his servant. "Acheng, show Mr. Morris out."

As the old servant approached, a sudden curiosity prompted me to ask, "Mr. Darcy, what about your family? Do they also reside here?"

With a serene smile, he replied, "I have no family. It's just Acheng and me here."

I exited without further comment, but as I reached the threshold, I turned back. "Mr. Darcy, I may visit again in the coming days."

His brow furrowed briefly, signaling reluctance, yet he courteously said, "You're welcome to return anytime."

As I left, I couldn't shake the feeling that the truth was as elusive as the mist that clung to the mountains around Fludent Garden.

I thanked Max Darcy and made my way to the gate, with Acheng, the old servant, trailing behind to see me out. As the gate shut with a resonant thud, I walked to my car, the enigma of the place gnawing at my thoughts, growing more intense with every step.

The vastness of the garden and the meticulous maintenance it required seemed improbable for just two residents. How could Acheng, tending to such extensive grounds, have been close enough to hear my knock at the gate? The sound of the copper ring was loud, true, but if they were both ensconced in the house, how would they have known of my arrival?

This inconsistency fueled my suspicion that Max Darcy was concealing something. I felt as though a veil had been drawn, obfuscating truths I was desperate to uncover.

As I settled into the driver's seat, a weary sigh escaped me. Why did it seem that everyone had secrets sequestered away? Jude Bailey had always exuded an air of mystery, and now Max Darcy echoed that same enigmatic aura.

Though I lacked tangible evidence to substantiate my suspicions, my intuition screamed otherwise, a persistent whisper that something was amiss.

Driving back to the city, my mind wandered. Once the sprawling estate of Fludent Garden disappeared from my rearview, questions lingered like ghosts. Max Darcy was undoubtedly affluent and seemingly content in his luxurious seclusion. Why then would he embark on constructing a building in the urban sprawl?

Another sigh broke the silence. Questions multiplied like fractals, yet the immediate priority was Steve Bond's disappearance. Perhaps the skepticism of my colleagues was warranted; perhaps I had veered off course, chasing phantoms in a labyrinth of conjecture while Steve Bond remained lost.

Back in the bustling city, I navigated through a sea of cars and pedestrians, eventually reaching Steve Bond's detective agency. As I entered, a chorus of greetings met me, indicating a development awaited my attention.

"What's happened?" I asked, sensing urgency in their voices.

"Colonel Jack from the police has been trying to reach you—called 17 or 18 times," one staff member reported. "He wants to meet."

My eyebrows arched in surprise. "Did he mention why?"

"No," another staff member replied, "but we uncovered that the building manager, Rory, is dead."

The news hit like a jolt of electricity. Rory's death was a grim escalation in an already tangled affair. "The colonel is at the building now. He needs you to come immediately," the staffer continued.

Without hesitation, I turned on my heel and departed, urgency driving my every move.

What began with a fright had spiraled into disappearance, and now, death—a trajectory that was rapidly intensifying. My nerves were taut as I maneuvered through traffic, the blare of my horn a constant companion. As I raced up the incline toward the building, my speed surprised even myself, propelled by the urgency of unraveling a mystery that seemed to deepen with each passing moment.

71

Chapter 5

Administrator's Mysterious Death

As I parked my car, the scene before me was a chaotic tapestry of flashing lights and official vehicles—police cars, ambulances, and ominous black vans clustered around the building's entrance. The air was tense, charged with the gravity of unfolding events.

A police officer approached, radio in hand, and spoke into it, "Colonel, Mr. Morris has arrived." The device crackled with Colonel Jack's voice, urging my swift ascent, "Send him up immediately!"

Momentarily taken aback, I asked, "Where is the colonel?"

The officer gestured upwards, "He's on the rooftop."

I stepped back and squinted against the sun, making out small figures silhouetted against the sky atop the building.

Through the distance, I discerned Colonel Jack, a tiny figure waving me up. Without delay, I entered the lobby and made my way to the elevator alongside the officer.

"Was the body found on the rooftop?" I inquired as we ascended.

"Yes," the officer confirmed. "A friend of Rory's came looking for him, noticed his absence, and checked the rooftop. He found the body and called the police."

A frown creased my forehead. "Why does the colonel need me?"

The officer shrugged, offering no answers. I watched the elevator's numbers blink steadily as we climbed, the anticipation thickening. Soon, we reached the top floor.

Exiting the elevator, Colonel Jack's voice boomed across the rooftop, "Ash, where have you been? I've been trying to reach you!"

I replied with a wry smile as I climbed the stairs, "Perhaps you should hone telepathy, Colonel. It would save us all some time."

Reaching the rooftop, Colonel Jack greeted me with a vigorous handshake, one that always made me suspect he was contemplating tossing me over the edge for sport, albeit with a laugh. Today, his expression was one of grim determination.

The rooftop was crowded with officials and personnel. Jack led me to the edge, where a body lay beneath a white cloth. He pulled back the cover, revealing Rory's remains. Despite my resolve, a chill coursed through me. The sight was unsettling.

Jack replaced the cloth and turned to me, his voice grim. "So, how did he die?"

I was momentarily speechless, glancing skyward in a futile search for answers. The sky offered no insights, just an expanse of blue. Jack, understanding my gesture, pressed on, "Any thoughts on what happened?"

Regaining composure, I asked, "Has the body been moved?"

Jack shook his head. "No, the evidence suggests he died right here. No signs of the body being moved."

The logic was irrefutable, yet reality seemed to defy explanation. "But that's impossible!" I exclaimed. "He fell from a height!"

I gestured at Rory's broken form. The injuries — shattered limbs—were unmistakable indicators of a fall from a great height. Yet, we were already atop a building over twenty stories high.

The absurdity of it gnawed at me. If Rory had fallen from above, where had he fallen from? The skies? The enigma twisted my thoughts in knots, compelling me to shake my head in disbelief.

Colonel Jack's bitter smile mirrored my own frustration. "I called you because we both reached the same impossible conclusion."

I asserted, "Anyone can see he fell from a significant height!"

The colonel nodded, "The forensic pathologist agrees. Even a fall from this rooftop to the ground wouldn't result in such injuries. It's as if he fell from much higher."

I looked up again, my mind grappling with the paradox. "Where could he have fallen from?"

Jack's hand gripped my shoulder, his voice laced with irony, "Perhaps a plane or helicopter passed overhead, and Rory fell from it."

I shook my head, humorless in the face of the grim impossibility. "Let's not jest, Colonel. Neither of us is in the mood for laughter."

As we stood there, the sky vast and indifferent above us, I realized we were on the cusp of something far stranger than anything we could have anticipated.

The colonel's sigh was filled with the weight of perplexity. "That's exactly why I needed to find you, Ash. It's so bizarre!" His words mirrored the confusion swirling in my own mind, reminiscent of what Jude Bailey had described — the elevator's endless ascent, the gray void above and below. I shared my thoughts with the colonel, pondering aloud: if someone had stepped off the balcony in such a state, where would they have fallen?

The colonel listened, his expression skeptical yet intrigued. "Are you suggesting that the elevator somehow rose beyond the physical limits of the building?"

"At least, that's what Jude Bailey's experience suggests," I replied.

Colonel Jack shook his head, "But Jude Bailey returned safely—he was still within the building."

I, too, shook my head, matching his bitter smile. "And yet, are we to believe the elevator extends upward, making the building grow?"

The colonel countered firmly, "There might have been a pause during the elevator's ascent, giving the impression of continuous movement."

I pressed the question, "But then, where did Rory fall from?"

The conversation was interrupted by the arrival of the forensic doctor and a police officer, who whispered updates to the colonel. With a nod, he signaled for the stretcher, and Rory's body was carefully lifted and taken away. The crimson stain it left behind confirmed the grim reality: Rory had indeed fallen from above, meeting his end upon the rooftop.

I pressed my temples, trying to clear the fog clouding my thoughts, but clarity remained elusive.

Colonel Jack turned to me, his tone shifting to professional pragmatism. "Ash, the police can't pursue a speculative investigation..."

I understood his unspoken request. "As before, I'll handle a private investigation, with your department's cooperation."

He nodded, and impulsively, I declared, "First, I need to speak with Jude Bailey again."

The colonel hesitated, "Is that really necessary?"

"Absolutely," I insisted. "Three individuals have had strange experiences in that elevator: Jude Bailey, Steve Bond, and now Rory."

Jack nodded, "True. Rory is dead, Steve Bond is missing, and Jude Bailey is our only lead."

"Exactly," I said. "I suspect Jude Bailey withheld something important about what happened after he exited the elevator."

The colonel paced, weighing my words. "He did accuse you of harassment last time. Let us arrange the meeting. Just be cautious—we have no hard evidence against him."

I conceded, "Understood, but I'm concerned it may not yield much."

With another heavy sigh, the colonel looked skyward, his thoughts likely echoing my own: where had Rory fallen from?

I lingered only briefly on the rooftop before taking my leave. Instead of returning to Steve Bond's detective agency, I sought solace in a place known for its tranquility—the "Silent Club." Here, silence was not just a rule but a prerequisite.

In the serene, elegantly adorned confines of the Silent Club, I found a sanctuary amidst the chaos that had become my thoughts. The patrons around me were as silent as statues, each lost in their own world, oblivious to the others. I settled into a plush sofa in the corner, cradling my head in my hands, attempting to untangle the web of confusion.

However, clarity eluded me. My mind was a jumbled mess, and even my usual method of distilling complex issues into manageable summaries failed me. The situation defied logic. The notion of an elevator transcending the physical limits of a building was absurd. Yet, it was upon this premise that I had based my entire investigation.

As I dwelled on this impossibility, a sudden epiphany struck me like a bolt of lightning, causing an involuntary shiver to ripple through my body.

Could it be that I had been misled from the start? If the "strange elevator" phenomenon was a fabrication, then my entire line of inquiry had been fundamentally flawed.

The haunting possibility loomed large: what if Jude Bailey had deceived us all? His account had been the cornerstone of my investigation. If his story was false, then I had been chasing shadows.

I sat up straight, my eyes wide with realization. In any other setting, this sudden movement might have drawn concerned inquiries, but here, in the Silent Club, no one disturbed my solitude.

If Jude Bailey's narrative was indeed a fabrication, then what was his motive? Perhaps he had genuinely experienced something in the elevator but chose to veil the truth with the fantastical tale of endless ascent.

By concocting the impossible story of the "rising elevator," he effectively redirected scrutiny. Experts would dismiss it as a psychological illusion, diverting attention from whatever truly transpired within those elevator walls.

This revelation sent a thrill of excitement coursing through me. Yet, it also raised further questions: what had Steve Bond encountered in the elevator?

Did Steve Bond's experience mirror Jude Bailey's? If so, why had Steve Bond disappeared while Jude Bailey emerged seemingly unscathed?

The Silent Club had given me time to reflect, but it was clear that my previous approach was flawed. The tangled web of contradictions needed untangling, and I was determined to get to the bottom of it. After leaving the club, I called Colonel Jack, who informed me of a meeting with Jude Bailey at 7 p.m. in his office. The hours leading up to it were spent in restless anticipation.

Arriving at the colonel's office, I was greeted with a firm handshake. Jack warned me that Jude Bailey might be averse to my questioning, suggesting that my approach might yield little. I was taken aback by his skepticism. "But I need to ask him," I insisted. "I suspect everything he's told us is fabricated."

Jack's expression revealed his dissatisfaction, yet he urged, "Whatever the case, approach him gently."

I couldn't help but bristle at the suggestion. "Do I look like a pirate?" I retorted, just as a police officer ushered in Jude Bailey. Jack turned his attention to our guest.

Upon seeing me, Jude Bailey's demeanor shifted to one of unease. He tried to focus on Jack's explanations, but his eyes kept darting toward me, filled with a mix of hostility and apprehension.

Seizing an opportune pause in the colonel's briefing, I interjected, "Mr. Bailey, do you recall Rory, the building manager?"

Jude Bailey's response was stiff, his body language betraying tension. "Yes, I remember."

"Rory is dead," I stated bluntly, "murdered."

Jude Bailey's reaction was a rehearsed display of shock, and the colonel shot me a reproachful glare. I understood his concern; "murder" was a heavy word without clear evidence. But I had a purpose: to instill the gravity of the situation in Jude Bailey, to urge him to think twice before weaving more tales.

Ignoring the colonel's disapproval, I presented a photo of Rory's lifeless body on the rooftop. Jude Bailey glanced at it briefly before looking away, murmuring, "Too horrifying."

"Rory fell from a height," I continued, watching for any tells in his reaction.

He looked again at the photo, puzzled. "Fell from a height? But he died on the rooftop."

I couldn't suppress a sardonic laugh. "Indeed, he did. And there are no signs his body was moved. This so-called 'murder' conveniently supports your story of an endlessly rising elevator."

Jude Bailey's complexion paled, his mouth opening and closing without sound. His discomfort was palpable, and I pressed on.

"I believe Rory's death is connected to you, Mr. Bailey."

In a flash, Jude Bailey was on his feet, addressing Jack with indignation, "What is this? Are the police accusing me? I'll bring in my lawyer!"

Jack quickly intervened, calming him, but not without casting a stern look my way. Once Jude Bailey was seated, Jack expressed disapproval. "Ash, that was too much."

I shrugged, unrepentant. "I never accused him of murder, only that there's a connection. No need to be defensive."

"What connection?" Jude Bailey demanded, his voice steely.

"That depends on your true experience in the building, Mr. Bailey," I replied evenly.

His anger flared again. "I've already told you what happened!"

"You claimed the elevator ascended for 20 minutes. But that's impossible."

Jude Bailey's face reddened. "Perhaps it was an illusion. I don't know if it stopped halfway."

I pointed at him accusingly. "You know more than you're telling us."

Jude Bailey slapped my hand away, exclaiming, "Absurdity! Why are the police wasting time on this nonsense? I'm leaving!"

He turned to go, but I called after him, "Mr. Bailey, Rory is dead, and Mr. Bond is missing. Consider your position carefully."

I had no solid evidence, but the air was thick with the scent of something sinister. I believed Jude Bailey had lied or omitted crucial details, possibly under duress. My words struck a nerve.

As Jude Bailey reached the door, he collided with it with a loud thud, an act of panic betraying his shock. My instincts were right; there was more beneath the surface.

I pressed once more, "It's in your best interest to tell us the truth."

Colonel Jack watched with a mixture of curiosity and concern as Jude Bailey turned back to face us, his facade crumbling.

Jude Bailey's pale face and the red mark on his forehead told a story of their own. When he turned to face me, his eyes blinked rapidly, a telltale sign of shock and inner turmoil he couldn't hide.

I maintained my composure, watching him with a cool detachment. Colonel Jack, though not entirely approving of my approach, was silent, hoping my tactics might yield some truth from Jude Bailey.

After a tense silence, Jude Bailey finally spoke, his voice dry and strained, "Do you expect the same tragedy to happen to me as well?"

I was ready. "That depends entirely on what really happened to you," I replied, my words measured and deliberate.

Jude Bailey seemed to regain some composure, sneering as he said, "I have no idea what you're insinuating."

After a tense silence, Jude Bailey finally spoke, his voice dry and strained, "Do you expect the same tragic happen to me as well?"

I was ready. "That depends entirely on what really happened to you," I replied, my words measured and deliberate.

Jude Bailey seemed to regain some composure, sneering as he said, "I have no idea what you're insinuating."

He paused, wiped his face, and added, "You're making something out of nothing."

I remained unfazed, responding, "I'm not fabricating anything. A person is missing, and another is dead."

His demeanor grew colder as he retorted, "People disappear and die every day."

"But not everyone is linked to that building or that elevator," I countered, my gaze unwavering.

Jude Bailey said nothing more, his eyes drifting away from mine. He asked Colonel Jack, "Can I leave?"

Jack, maintaining his professional demeanor, replied, "Mr. Bailey, we invited you here to help us understand what happened. Any information could be invaluable."

With a calm but firm tone, Jude Bailey repeated, "I've already shared everything about that day."

Jack glanced at me, and with a resigned smile, I nodded. "You're free to go, Mr. Bailey, but your continued cooperation would be greatly appreciated," Jack said.

Jude Bailey scoffed, turned, and left, this time without incident.

Once he was gone, Jack turned to me with a hint of frustration. "What did you hope to achieve with that approach?"

"At the very least," I replied, "I'm more convinced than ever that he's hiding something."

Jack couldn't argue with that. Jude Bailey's reaction to my bluff had been telling—panic often betrays secrets.

I assured Jack, "Don't worry, I'll handle this. The key to unraveling it all lies with him."

Jack sighed, his reluctance evident. "Fine, but tread carefully. Legally, he's in a strong position."

I nodded, acknowledging the truth in his words. "I'll be cautious."

With a new plan in mind, I left Jack's office. The next day, I assembled a team of five skilled detectives from Steve Bond's agency. Together, we formed a rotating watch on Jude Bailey, monitoring him around the clock.

Equipped with radios courtesy of Jack, we maintained constant communication, ready to relay any developments.

Four days passed without any breakthroughs. Despite our vigilance, Jude Bailey's activities revealed nothing suspicious. Meanwhile, Steve Bond remained missing. Every resource had been deployed in the search, yet there was no trace of him. The longer his absence stretched, the more I feared for his safety.

I couldn't bear to face Mrs. Bond, knowing I might have to deliver the worst news imaginable.

With a murder clouding the building's reputation, the police presence was constant. Max Darcy, the owner, was surprisingly accommodating, allowing the police to maintain their watch. He seemed indifferent, knowing the building would languish on the market regardless.

Amidst these shadows, the truth remained elusive, yet I felt a relentless pull toward uncovering the secrets hidden within that elevator and the building's walls.

Chapter 6

Twice the Mistakes

In the labyrinthine cityscape, where the hum of daily life blended seamlessly into the background, Jude Bailey's existence unfolded with a banal predictability, as if scripted by some unseen hand. Each morning, he embarked on his commute, immersing himself in the monotony of work, only to surface briefly for a midday meal at a nearby eatery. By evening, he returned to the solitude of his dwelling. Occasionally, he ventured out to engage in the societal rituals of entertainment or leisure—a walk, a film perhaps—but his life remained a testament to the crushing regularity that defined so many. It was a chilling thought, to witness and record such unvaried existence, yet it mirrored the lives of countless others.

The fifth day of this unremarkable surveillance was a Sunday, a day when the world seemed to exhale. I was at the brink of abandoning my quest. Jude Bailey's trail had led to naught but dead ends. Yet, there was no other path, no other lead, and so, with reluctant resolve, I continued. That morning, as the first light filtered through the curtains, Flora opened our door to an unexpected visitor—Mrs. Bond.

The woman was a portrait of tension and urgency, though subtly altered from the distraught figure I had encountered in the wake of Steve Bond's inexplicable disappearance. Her eyes found mine, and her voice, tinged with desperation, declared, "Mr. Morris, I received a call from him!"

The room seemed to contract around me. The "him" was unmistakably Steve Bond, whose vanishing act had woven a tapestry of enigma and speculation. The mere mention of his call sent a shiver of excitement through me.

"Where is he?" I demanded, the words tumbling out before I could restrain them.

Mrs. Bond shook her head, her expression a mosaic of confusion and hope. "I don't know. His words were strange, but it was his voice—I'm sure of it."

In her hand was a small tape recorder, an anachronism in this digital age, yet a guardian of secrets. "Since the trouble began, I've feared the worst. I record every call," she explained, urgency quickening her speech. "Please, listen. This came just twenty minutes ago. I rushed here the moment it ended."

I accepted the tape recorder, pressed play, and let the machine weave its narrative. Steve Bond's voice, a spectral echo of familiarity, emerged from the static—a voice I had known for over a decade. It was undeniably his, yet it sounded distorted, as though some distance, both physical and metaphysical, lay between us. The cadence was elongated, the pitch altered, as if the very fabric of sound had been stretched thin.

"Do you hear my voice? Can you hear me?" His voice droned, a question suspended in time.

Mrs. Bond's reply was urgent, pleading. "I hear you! Where are you? Why is your voice so slow?"

Steve Bond continued, oblivious to her query, "I'm fine, you needn't worry. I will return. I'm trying to come back."

Her voice broke with emotion, a cry of desperation. "Where are you? Tell me!"

But Steve Bond remained locked in his own narrative, a monologue that eerily aligned with her questions. "I don't know where I am," he confessed, "It's strange here, everything is strange. But rest assured, I will come back. I will definitely come back."

The recording ended in a chorus of Mrs. Bond's frantic "Hello?" and the finality of silence.

I replayed the tape, my mind a storm of conjecture. Mrs. Bond's eyes beseeched me for answers I could not provide. "Where is he?" she implored, tears tracing paths down her cheeks.

I offered a wry smile, heavy with uncertainty. "Even he doesn't know. How could we?"

Flora, ever perceptive, interjected, "The words weren't spoken live. It sounds as if someone recorded his message first and played it over the phone at double speed."

Her insight was a beacon cutting through the fog. I adjusted the playback speed of the tape recorder and listened anew. This time, Steve Bond's voice emerged clearly, while Mrs. Bond's words came through in a rapid staccato. Flora's deduction held undeniable merit.

We listened again, and again, each repetition a plunge into the depths of mystery. Mrs. Bond's question lingered in the air, "Why doesn't he tell us where he is?"

The conundrum gnawed at me, but I offered what comfort I could. "If he truly is safe, as he insists, then perhaps we should not worry unduly."

Mrs. Bond voiced a fear that echoed my own. "What if it's just a recording, not him at all?"

I understood her dread, yet I cut in with a calm I did not feel. "There are two possibilities: he is under duress, in which case contact will be made again. Or, he has experienced something beyond our understanding, and he will reach out once more."

Turning to Flora, I said, "Please accompany Mrs. Bond back. She shouldn't be alone."

Flora nodded, departing with Mrs. Bond, leaving me to my thoughts. I sought out Jack, replaying the tape for him, searching for clarity amidst the chaos.

"If it was pre-recorded," I mused, "why slow it down?"

Jack pondered, "If not a recording, altering one's voice is no small feat. Manipulating sound waves is another matter entirely."

A sense of significance loomed, tantalizingly close yet elusive. The colonel, with a resigned chuckle, remarked, "Let's hope he calls home again soon."

The bitter smile that crept across my face was a mask for the tumult within. The situation had spiraled into the absurd, yet I clung to the thread of hope that Steve Bond was alive. This revelation, amidst the chaos, was a singular point of solace.

Engaging in a terse dialogue with Colonel Jack, I was abruptly interrupted by the static-laden "zizi" of the radio at my side. Adjusting the antenna, I strained to catch the garbled transmission. The report came through, clear enough: "Jude Bailey's family has left home — they're heading out, likely for an outing."

Without hesitation, I commanded, "Follow him!"

Colonel Jack, with a weary shake of his head, questioned my persistence. "Still chasing leads with Jude Bailey?"

I spread my hands in a gesture of helplessness. "Is there another path to pursue?"

Jack sighed, recounting the events etched into memory. "Remember, after the accident, Jude Bailey's terror-stricken confession about the elevator—it was genuine. No one could fabricate such horror."

I remained silent, my thoughts a tangled web.

Jack continued, "And Steve Bond, as you described—driven to flee in panic. Such a reaction isn't conjured from mere imagination."

"True," I conceded slowly. "I don't dispute the terror they faced. What nags at me is the suspicion that Jude Bailey isn't entirely truthful. Either he's concocted a story to mask his true ordeal, or he's only revealing fragments, concealing crucial details."

Jack relented with a nod. "Very well, the decision is yours. At least we have confirmation that Mr. Bond is alive."

"Yes," I murmured, "but the question remains—where is he, truly? His cryptic call provided no answers. Is he held captive, unaware of his own location?"

Jack dismissed the notion with a wave. "He never mentioned imprisonment — just that he's in a bizarre situation."

There was little more to be said. The puzzle pieces we possessed were insufficient to form any coherent picture.

Leaving the colonel's office, I spent the following hour absorbing updates on Jude Bailey's movements. His family's leisurely drive to the suburbs seemed innocuous—a typical family retreat. Initially.

But as the reports continued, a subtle unease settled over me. The path they traversed was leading them towards something noteworthy—"Fludent Garden."

The unusual destination stirred my instincts. I instructed the tail to increase vigilance. Twenty minutes later, a new report arrived: Jude Bailey and his family, picnicking in a clearing near Fludent Garden. All seemed ordinary, unremarkable.

Then came a report that ignited my pulse. Jude Bailey, under the guise of nonchalance, had slipped away from his family, briskly approaching the gates of Fludent Garden. The observer noted that as he reached the entrance, it swung open as if anticipating his arrival.

The revelation sent a thrill through me. Jude Bailey was clandestinely linked to Max Darcy, the enigmatic owner of the garden. Their connection was shrouded in secrecy, else why this elaborate ruse to mask their meeting?

Initially, I resolved to dash to Fludent Garden, but caution prevailed. Alerting them prematurely could jeopardize everything.

The operative's assurance that photos had been taken was my solace. I awaited further updates with bated breath.

Jude Bailey's visit to Fludent Garden was fleeting — ten minutes, a sliver of time.

In those ten minutes, much could transpire, yet little could physically occur. The layout of Fludent Garden was etched in my memory—it would take the entirety of those ten minutes simply to traverse from gate to villa. This implied that the person Jude Bailey sought was stationed immediately beyond the threshold, awaiting his arrival.

As evening fell, the tracking personnel were replaced, and Jude Bailey returned to the city. The photos were developed quickly, capturing a continuous sequence. Six photos showed Jude Bailey entering Fludent Garden, and another six documented his exit.

In the series of photos, Jude Bailey appeared to almost "rush" into Fludent Garden. He sprinted towards the gate, which seemed half-closed as if anticipating his arrival. His haste suggested secrecy—perhaps he didn't want his family, who were picnicking nearby, to notice his brief absence.

When Jude Bailey emerged, his head was bowed, burdened with thoughts. This was evident in the consecutive photos, capturing a man deep in contemplation.

Questions swirled in my mind. Why would Jude Bailey and Max Darcy have a secret meeting? I assumed Jude Bailey went to Fludent Garden to see Max Darcy.

There was no apparent connection between the two. The only link was that Jude Bailey had experienced something strange and terrifying in the building Max Darcy had constructed.

Why would Jude Bailey want to meet Max Darcy? The best course of action was to find Jude Bailey and get answers.

However, past encounters had taught me of his aversion towards me, his determination to guard his secrets. Even the photographic evidence might fail to breach his defenses if he fabricated another tale in response.

Pondering my next move, I found myself alone in Steve Bond's dimly lit detective agency. The clatter of typewriters had long ceased. I checked the radio once more; Jude Bailey had retreated to the safety of his home.

Resolving to act boldly, I dialed Jude Bailey's number, a plan forming—a gamble that could unravel the truth, if only my assumptions held firm.

The assumption was simple, yet profound: Jude Bailey had indeed gone to meet with Max Darcy.

The phone rang, its tone a metronome marking time, until finally, a voice answered — Jude Bailey's voice, unmistakable in its timbre. I cloaked my voice in age and gravitas, speaking with careful authority, "Mr. Bailey, I understand you met with Mr. Darcy this afternoon. He has asked me to contact you."

Silence greeted my words, a pause pregnant with uncertainty. I imagined Jude Bailey caught in a moment of disorientation. When he finally spoke, it was with a reluctance that only confirmed my suspicion. "What's the issue? We settled things earlier."

His response was a revelation, a confirmation that my hunch had landed squarely on the truth.

Pressing my advantage, I continued, urgency lacing my words, "It's crucial, Mr. Bailey. It won't take long. I need to see you. There's something important that can't be discussed over the phone. Meet me at the September Coffee Shop in thirty minutes. Look for the man with a book."

I concluded the call abruptly, leaving him no room for doubt or denial, confident he would come.

My instincts were validated; Jude Bailey had indeed met with Max Darcy that afternoon. I felt certain he would appear at our rendezvous.

Within Steve Bond's makeup arsenal, I transformed myself into an elderly figure, the disguise complete in a mere ten minutes. I then made my way to the September Coffee House.

This venue was notorious for its atmosphere—dimly lit, with towering chairs creating pockets of privacy. It was a perfect venue for anonymity, ensuring Jude Bailey would struggle to discern my true identity.

Settled in the coffee house, I saw Jude Bailey enter after a mere five minutes. I lifted my book, signaling him, and he approached, taking a seat across from me.

Our eyes met, a silent duel of recognition and concealment. He broke the silence first, his words laced with defiance, "How long do you plan to control me?"

His choice of words—"control"—was a red flag, evidence of the gravity of his situation.

I replied with measured calm, "Mr. Bailey, you've suffered no harm."

His response was sharp, bitten off with frustration. "No harm? In your eyes, maybe. But I've had enough. Am I just a guinea pig to you?"

"Guinea pig"—another term loaded with implications that left me momentarily speechless.

Regaining composure, I ventured, "Compared to others, you're in a better position than Mr. Bond."

This was a gamble. If Steve Bond's situation differed from Jude Bailey's, my facade could crumble instantly. The tension in that moment was palpable.

Jude Bailey's expression shifted to one of resignation. "I've accepted Mr. Darcy's explanation. He's made two mistakes already. I won't be a victim of a third."

His confession was a windfall. The "two mistakes" likely referred to Rory and Steve Bond, and the orchestrator of these errors was "Mr. Darcy"—Max Darcy. This link was invaluable.

I realized my assumed identity was Max Darcy's envoy, and so I played my part, responding with a series of dry laughs.

Jude Bailey's anger simmered, "I can't control what he does, nor do I want to."

I pressed further, my tone icy, "Then why venture to the countryside to see him?"

His face darkened, words emerging as a reluctant murmur, "I shouldn't have accepted his money."

His admission was electrifying. Max Darcy had paid Jude Bailey—a bribe, surely. But for what purpose?

As my mind raced, Jude Bailey, perhaps lost in his own turmoil, continued without noticing my silence. "Everyone wants money, and he pays so well."

I seized the moment, echoing his sentiment, "So, Mr. Bailey, follow Mr. Darcy's instructions, gain wealth, and comply with his benefit."

His response was bitter, "Follow his instructions? If he errs again, I'll be the victim. What's the point of the money then?"

His words were laden with implication.

Analyzing the conversation, I pieced together a narrative. Max Darcy had paid Jude Bailey not just for silence, but to undertake a task—one fraught with peril.

This task was dangerous. Like Rory and Steve Bond, money would be meaningless if things went awry.

It seemed today's meeting between Max Darcy and Jude Bailey had soured, perhaps leading Jude Bailey to reject Darcy's demands. My impersonation of Max Darcy's representative was fortuitous, unveiling truths otherwise hidden.

With these insights, I challenged him, my voice cold and probing, "So, would you return the money, then?"

In the dim glow of the café, Jude Bailey's eyes bore into me, a volatile mix of surprise and anger contorting his face. His voice cut through the ambient chatter, sharp and slicing, "What do you mean by saying that? Did Mr. Darcy tell you? Don't forget, his secret is still in my hands!"

My pulse quickened, a staccato rhythm of adrenaline and anticipation. So it was true—Max Darcy harbored a secret, and Jude Bailey, the ever-enigmatic puppet master, had strings tied to it. My suspicions, long nurtured in the shadows of my mind, now stood validated in the glaring light of revelation. He was indeed cloaked in secrets, those of Max Darcy, never whispered to another soul.

An inexpressible thrill surged through me, igniting a firestorm of thoughts on how to pry this clandestine knowledge from Jude Bailey's grasp. But before my mental machinations could take shape, a voice, deep and resonant, emerged from behind, "Mr. Bailey, even if I have a secret in your hands, you don't have to tell everyone!"

Recognition struck like lightning. I sprang from my seat, Max Darcy's voice unmistakable. A hand clamped onto my shoulder, a touch too familiar, too restraining. Instinct and resolve merged as I brushed it aside with a swift motion, pivoting to face the source with determined swiftness.

There he stood, Max Darcy, his presence solid and unyielding. Though his sighting was inconsequential to my identity, an unbidden impulse propelled my fist forward, a reflexive response to his encroachment. My knuckles met his face with deliberate force—not enough to maim, but sufficient to unbalance him, sending him collapsing to the floor.

Without hesitation, I bolted for the exit, the café's sudden uproar fading in my wake. I sprinted into the anonymity of the street, calculating each step to ensure by the time pursuit began, I'd be lost to their eyes, disappearing around the next corner.

This immediate departure was necessary to preserve my anonymity. With my identity veiled, I could confront Jude Bailey anew, in daylight, under the guise of civility. I'd listen to his fabrications and, with strategic timing, unveil the truth, forcing his hand to reveal the depths of his deceit.

My conviction in this strategy was unwavering, even as the night unraveled in ways unforeseen.

Returning home, exhilaration buzzed through my veins. The puzzle pieces were aligning, the murky waters clearing. In the labyrinth of unsolved mysteries, the first clue often heralds the unraveling of the entire enigma. What might torment for years could unravel in mere days once the thread is found.

Despite the late hour, sleep eluded me, anticipation pulsating with each tick of the clock. Morning brought with it the mundane ritual of the newspaper, scanning for whispers of the previous night's altercation. Yet, predictably, the world spun on, indifferent to our small café skirmish.

Time marched on, and by now, Jude Bailey should have been ensconced within his office walls. I dialed his company, expecting routine, but was met with the unexpected: "Director Bailey didn't come to work today."

My disbelief hung in the air, "Did he ask for leave?"

"No," came the curt reply. "We called his home, and his wife said he didn't come back last night."

The words hung, heavy and disconcerting. "Didn't come back? What do you mean, where is he?"

Impatience tinged the response, "We don't know. His family doesn't know either, so we've called the police."

The line went dead, leaving me with a cold receiver and colder realization — Jude Bailey, the man of meticulous routine, had vanished into the night.

Days of observation had painted Jude Bailey as a creature of habit, his life a predictable pattern. Yet now, he was a specter, his absence an enigma that defied the boundaries of what I thought I understood.

Chapter 7

The Truth Is Dawning

In the quiet aftermath of chaos, I reached for the radio, the weight of last night's events pressing heavily on my mind. Disguised and incognito, I had posed as Max Darcy's representative for a clandestine rendezvous with Jude Bailey—a secret kept from all. Yet, the eyes that monitored Jude Bailey's every move would surely have noted his disappearance, given that our meeting unfolded under their watchful surveillance.

With urgency, I pressed the intercom button, my voice sharp with impatience, "Who is following Jude Bailey now?"

Silence greeted my inquiries, a void both unsettling and foreboding. Just then, the phone intruded with a sudden ring. Colonel Jack's voice, authoritative and brisk, crackled through the receiver, "Ash, Jude Bailey is missing!"

My response came on a breath, "I know. I was just about to track him down. He hasn't returned home."

The colonel's tone grew grave, "Staying out all night is trivial. I fear he's met with an accident."

A chill laced my spine. "Why are you so certain?"

He snorted, a sound of both frustration and confirmation, "Aren't you and others tailing Jude Bailey around the clock?"

"Yes," I conceded, "I tried to reach them just now, but couldn't. Do you have any news?"

His voice carried a grim note, "The operative shadowing Jude Bailey last night was shot in the head at midnight, left unconscious on the road. Passers-by summoned an ambulance, and he's currently in the hospital. I'm here now. Do you want to come?"

"I'll be there in ten minutes. Which hospital?" He provided the details, and I was off, urgency propelling me forward.

I rushed out the door, heading straight there. I hurried upstairs and in a corridor, I saw Jack and several senior police officers discussing with a doctor. As I approached, I heard the doctor say, "He's still very weak and has lost a lot of blood. Don't trouble him for too long."

The colonel nodded, turned around, glanced at me, and snorted. I angrily retorted, "What are you humming about? It's not my fault."

Jack shouted, "Track and monitor Jude Bailey, isn't that your idea."

I was both angry and amused. "Damn it, he's gone missing even under surveillance. If we hadn't tracked him, he'd have disappeared without a trace and we'd have no clues!"

Jack rolled his eyes, momentarily at a loss for words. I said, "Forget it, let's hear what clues there are."

As I spoke, I pushed open the door to the ward.

I found the injured operative, Steve Bond's colleague, swathed in gauze, his pallor stark against the sterile white of the sheets. As I entered the ward, he trembled, a faint murmur escaping his lips, though indistinguishable.

Colonel Jack, having left the others outside, nodded for me to proceed. "Speak slowly," I urged, "there's no rush."

The staff member sighed, recounting, "Last night, I kept watch on Jude Bailey as usual. Around nine, he suddenly rushed out, and I trailed him."

A tension line creased my brow as he continued, "He led me to a dimly lit café, where someone awaited him."

Jack interjected, his curiosity piqued, "What did that person look like?"

The clerk's expression was bitter, "I managed to capture their meeting on a small camera, but after the attack, the camera vanished."

I waved off the inquiry, "No need to identify the person. Continue."

Of course, the identity was no mystery to me—I was the one who met Jude Bailey. The clerk inhaled deeply, resuming, "Jude Bailey and the stranger talked heatedly. Jude Bailey seemed agitated, but I couldn't discern their words."

"What happened after that?" I prodded, my own anxiety barely concealed.

The clerk hesitated, gauging my urgency with a questioning look, then continued, "Later, another man appeared—"

Colonel Jack interrupted, "Wait, you haven't described the first man."

The clerk struggled to recall, "It was dark, and I couldn't see clearly. I remember he had a somber look, and his height was similar to Mr. Morris's."

His observation was keen, having noted my height. The colonel pressed on, "And the man who came later?"

The clerk described, "He was older, of average build. As soon as he entered, he stood behind the stranger, placed a hand on his shoulder, and said something. The stranger abruptly stood, turned, and landed a punch. The older man fell, and then the stranger fled."

His account aligned perfectly with the events of last night in the café. Yet, what transpired after my hasty exit was uncharted territory.

The clerk added, "I immediately gave chase—"

Colonel Jack's voice resonated with a steely edge. "You shouldn't have chased him," he admonished the clerk, "Your duty was to monitor Jude Bailey."

The clerk blinked, a flicker of contrition crossing his features. "Yes, I chased him to the door but lost sight of the mysterious man. I returned immediately. The café was in disarray, waitstaff in a flurry, intent on calling the police. Yet, the man who joined later slipped them a banknote, and he spirited Jude Bailey away."

Colonel Jack and I exchanged a sharp intake of breath. "Did you continue to follow them?" the colonel pressed.

The clerk nodded, "Yes, I trailed them as they walked to another café, engaging in conversation for about an hour.

Jude Bailey exited first, his demeanor one of defeat. The older man followed shortly."

I interrupted, "Why didn't you follow Jude Bailey immediately?"

A shadow of regret clouded the clerk's face, "I'd tailed Jude Bailey for days without progress. I gambled on tracking the other man, thinking he might lead to a breakthrough."

A rueful smile tugged at my lips as he continued, "I followed the old man down a deserted street. My focus was ahead, unprepared for the blow that struck from behind. When consciousness returned, I found myself here, in the hospital."

Colonel Jack's gaze was a tangible weight, his tone icy, "Any leads?"

His words were a thinly veiled jab at my efforts, a reminder of the resources marshaled without result. I sidestepped his barb, addressing the clerk, "Rest well. The truth will surface soon."

The clerk's weary smile was tinged with skepticism, his exhaustion palpable. As Colonel Jack and I exited the ward, his critique resumed, cold and relentless, "Your words are comforting, though hollow without evidence."

Accustomed to his needling, I met his challenge with equal frost, "Colonel, what gives you the right to dismiss my assurance as mere platitude?"

His sneer was palpable, "Isn't it though? You claim proximity to a resolution without tangible proof."

I held his gaze, unyielding, "Colonel, how well do you grasp last night's events?"

His skepticism faltered in the face of my confidence. "I know what the clerk recounted. I suspect you know no more than I."

I chuckled, drawing his curiosity with a cryptic smile. My hand clapped his shoulder with camaraderie laced with irony, "I know far more, Colonel. Do you know who met Jude Bailey at the September Coffee House?"

His eyes flickered with incredulity, a question unspoken. "You know?"

"Indeed," I replied candidly, "because that mysterious figure was me."

Shock widened his eyes to saucers, his voice rising, "What were you doing?"

I gestured for quiet, "Lower your voice, Colonel. This is a hospital, after all."

His expression soured, his pride stung by my rebuke. Yet intrigue softened his glare as I elaborated on my motives for meeting Jude Bailey.

Despite his bluster, Colonel Jack was astute, swiftly pinpointing the heart of the matter, "Who was the man that followed?"

I prompted him to guess, and after a moment's contemplation, he ventured, "Max Darcy?"

"Precisely. Max Darcy, the puppet master pulling strings from the shadows of Fludent Garden. Everything spirals from his singular influence."

Understanding dawned, sweeping away the colonel's confusion as I recounted my conversation with Jude Bailey. Although Jude Bailey's whereabouts and the tragedy befalling Steve Bond and Rory remained shrouded in mystery, Max Darcy emerged as the linchpin.

Colonel Jack's excitement was palpable, his command decisive, "What are we waiting for? Let's issue an arrest warrant for Max Darcy!"

I tempered his enthusiasm, "We lack concrete evidence. Let's approach with diplomacy—invite or visit him for a conversation."

The colonel's anticipation was infectious, "Will you join me?"

After a moment's reflection, I agreed, "If it helps. My presence might deter any deceit."

With a nod of accord, Colonel Jack made several calls, mobilizing a formidable force. As we sped toward the suburbs, the scale of the operation became apparent. Police units dotted the highway like chess pieces in a calculated gambit. Reports flowed in, confirming Fludent Garden was encircled, yet undisturbed, its tranquility unmarred by the encroaching storm.

As Colonel Jack and I stepped out of the vehicle, the ensemble of senior officers emerged from their positions, briefing the colonel on the perimeter secured around Fludent Garden. I exchanged a knowing look with Jack, who quickly justified the heavy presence. "This isn't overkill," he asserted. "Max Darcy is pivotal. We cannot afford his escape."

I continued tapping at the heavy door, recalling the wait from my prior visit. After an agonizing three minutes, the small panel slid open, revealing the familiar visage of the old servant. Recognition flickered in his eyes. "Hello, Mr. Morris," he greeted.

I nodded, urgency in my tone. "I need to see your master. Please, open the door."

The servant hesitated, eyes darting nervously. "Mr. Morris, it's unfortunate timing. The master is away."

At this, Colonel Jack's patience snapped. He pushed forward, his voice booming, "When did he leave? Where to?"

The servant's gaze darted between me and the growing ranks of officers, alarmed. "Mr. Morris, what is happening?"

But Jack cut in, voice unyielding, "Answer the question!"

His authority compelled the servant to respond, albeit shakily. "He left for Penang, the day before yesterday."

My disbelief erupted, "Penang? Day before yesterday? That's a lie—I saw him just last night!"

The servant, bewildered, stammered, his confusion genuine. Meanwhile, Jack commanded, "Open the door. We have urgent matters to address. If he's hiding, we'll find him."

In legal terms, a search warrant should be required for entering the house. However, Colonel Jack clearly took advantage of the old servant, who didn't understand the protocols.

Reluctantly, the servant complied, and with that, the officers surged forward, sweeping into the garden. I found myself in agreement with Jack's earlier decision; Fludent Garden was vast—a veritable labyrinth that warranted such manpower.

The servant was visibly shaken, and I sought to reassure him with a gentle pat. "Don't worry. Your master is fine. I just have some questions. Now, tell me truthfully, where is he?"

Tears brimmed in the servant's eyes. "I drove him to the airport two days ago!"

I scoffed, "And yet, Mr. Bailey visited yesterday. You didn't happen to notice him, did you?"

His eyes widened in genuine surprise. "Mr. Bailey? I don't know any Mr. Bailey!"

With that, Jack and I pressed into the house, ignoring its opulent décor in our search. An hour passed fruitlessly, and frustration mounted. As Jack paced, a thought struck me, prompting a self-reproachful slap to my forehead. "We've been fools. We should check with the airline and immigration—see if Max Darcy truly left."

Jack's eyes narrowed. "You think I didn't consider that? But I trust your word—you claimed to have seen him last night."

I nodded, though my confidence wavered. "It's not mutually exclusive. He could have staged his departure and returned clandestinely."

Jack stepped out, his silence a testament to the gravity of the situation, utilizing a wireless link to reach headquarters. Fludent Garden, devoid of modernity, offered no conveniences—no doorbell, no phone, not even electric lights.

Half an hour later, Jack returned, his demeanor darkened. "What did you find?" I queried.

"Max Darcy boarded a flight to Penang the afternoon before yesterday," he reported, "He made appearances there, celebrated by the local elite, with records documenting his presence almost hourly. Ash, perhaps it's your eyesight that failed you."

The colonel's words stung, his skepticism dismissive of the truth I held resolute. Eye problems? Preposterous. I was certain—unwaveringly so—that the man I confronted was Max Darcy. His identity was clear, corroborated by both my recognition and Jude Bailey's. Despite Jack's derision, I clung to the facts I knew were unassailable.

The weight of the revelation settled heavily on my shoulders as I processed the undeniable fact that Max Darcy had indeed left for Penang, his trail marked by public appearances. Yet, my eyes had not deceived me; the man I encountered last night was undoubtedly him. Amidst this tangle of certainty and contradiction, Colonel Jack withdrew his forces, his frustration palpable. He issued stern warnings to the old servant about maintaining silence, wary of any legal repercussions should Max Darcy choose to contest the intrusion.

Colonel Jack's frustration was palpable, his orders to withdraw echoing sharply in the air. He stormed off, leaving me behind without a word or backward glance. My mind was a whirlwind of confusion, and I sat in a stupor, oblivious to the fact that the police had all departed.

When I finally snapped back to reality, I realized with a jolt that Colonel Jack and the entire contingent had been gone for at least thirty minutes. The cavernous, antique hall of Fludent Garden felt oppressively silent, with only the old servant remaining, his expression a mix of curiosity and concern as he lingered at the doorway. The stillness wrapped around us, thick and heavy.

With a resigned sigh, I managed a wry smile and rose to my feet. The old servant stepped forward, his movements quick and deliberate, as if eager to offer assistance or perhaps explanations.

"You live alone in such a vast place?" I inquired, more to fill the silence than out of genuine curiosity.

He nodded, a resigned acceptance in his voice. "I'm accustomed to it. Even when the master is here, he prefers silence, much like living alone."

Reflecting on his words, I wandered toward the exit, my mind a whirlwind of thoughts too tangled to unravel. The quiet of the surroundings amplified the sound of his footsteps trailing behind me. My mind was a cacophony of questions with no answers, a storm of confusion that compelled me to halt and turn abruptly.

The decision to turn was instinctual, unplanned. In that moment of pivoting, I caught sight of the old servant engaged in something decidedly odd. Though he ceased his actions the instant I turned, my eyes had registered the sight—a gleaming metal tube, slender and pen-like, poised in his hand.

The outer edge of the tube glinted, betraying a glass component. His swift concealment of the tube into his sleeve, executed with breathtaking precision, took less than a heartbeat—but I had seen it.

We stood frozen, the air between us charged with unspoken tension. His expression was a canvas of shock, painted with the realization that his secret had been inadvertently laid bare. His immobility was not calm but a paralysis of fear, a desperate uncertainty of how to proceed.

My mind raced as I grappled with the implications. I had overlooked the old servant, blinded by the apparent clarity that everything revolved around Max Darcy. Yet, the servant, residing in such close quarters, could hardly be ignorant of his master's secrets. Now, faced with this unexpected turn, I needed to tread carefully, avoiding any rash actions that might provoke an extreme response from him. This situation required a delicate touch, akin to rousing a sleepwalker teetering on the edge of a precipice.

After a tense half-minute, I spoke in a tone deliberately casual, "What is that?"

His reaction was immediate, visceral—he sprang forward as if prodded by an invisible blade, attempting to flee. Anticipating such a response, I moved with agility, intercepting him with a swift pivot. We collided, and I seized his arm.

His panic was palpable, compelling me to offer reassurance, "Stay calm. Whatever this is, we can talk it through."

Words failed him, his lips quivering with unspoken fear, while perspiration beaded on his forehead. Yet, as I observed closely, the sweat only emerged from the creases of his skin, the rest of his face strangely dry—a telltale sign of disguise. His face was a mask, painted with meticulous care.

Moreover, as I gripped his arm, the tautness of his muscles belied his apparent age. No elder could possess such vigor. This was no true old servant before me, but a young man shrouded in deception.

Chapter 8

Blinded by Assault

Understanding the gravity of the situation, I took a deep breath and tried to calm the young man masquerading as the old servant. "Don't be nervous, young man, don't be nervous," I reassured him.

His breath came in quick gasps, and I knew that he'd lost the will to resist once I saw through his disguise. I released my grip on his arm.

True to my expectations, he stood there, bewildered and unmoving. "Let's have a proper conversation," I suggested.

He struggled to find his voice, finally managing, "Mr. Morris, I admire you. I've heard much about you, and I know the kind of person you are—"

His words were disjointed, a testament to his shock. I placed a reassuring hand on his shoulder. "Stay calm. There's no need for panic."

Tears welled in his eyes as he confessed, "But someone died!"

I held his gaze. "Did you kill them?"

He shook his head vehemently, his entire demeanor one of horror. "Since you're not the killer, what frightens you?" I pressed.

"I'm scared. Please, I beg you, leave for now. Let me find you later today, once I've calmed down. I promise I'll contact you before dark," he pleaded.

I hesitated. His request was difficult to accept. Trusting him to follow through seemed risky, especially when he was my sole, crucial lead. How could I let him out of my sight?

Despite his earnestness, I steeled myself and shook my head. "No. We need to talk now, or we'll head to the police station together."

The mere mention of the police station caused him to recoil. "Why? Why is it necessary?" he muttered, almost to himself.

Ignoring his protests, I demanded, "Who is Max Darcy? Who are you?"

No answer.

"What are you doing here?"

Silence.

I raised my voice, "What was in your hand earlier?"

Still no response, but I didn't need one. I reached out and grabbed his arm again.

He recoiled, but I managed to catch his sleeve. We both exerted force, and with a rip, the sleeve tore away, revealing the metallic tube.

As I bent to retrieve it, I underestimated him. In my urgency, I forgot that cornered individuals might fight back. Something hard struck the back of my head with brutal force—not a mere fist.

The impact sent me sprawling, my vision swimming. Instinctively, I reached out, hooking his ankle as I fell. I think I took him down with me, but I couldn't be sure. The blow was too severe—I lost consciousness almost immediately.

When I came to, it felt as though a searing piece of metal burned at the back of my head. Opening my eyes yielded nothing but darkness, an absence of sight that was more than just the absence of light. Blindness.

Panicked, I cried out, struggling to sit up. Hands steadied me, and I recognized Colonel Jack's voice urging calm, "Steady, steady!"

"I can't see," I gasped, "I can't see anything!"

Jack maintained his grip, silent at first. When I called his name repeatedly, he finally explained, "The doctor predicted this. The head injury affected your optic nerve, but it might be temporary."

"What if it's permanent?" I screamed, fear giving way to desperation.

Jack didn't respond, and in my frustration, I lashed out, punching blindly. I connected with something—I heard the colonel's footsteps stumble back, followed by a crash.

Then, arms wrapped around me, and I heard Flora's voice, gentle but firm, "You can't just hit people!"

Grasping her hands tightly, I asked, my voice shaking, "Look at me—are my eyes open?"

Her voice trembled with restrained emotion. "Yes, they're wide open."

"Then why can't I see?" I shouted.

"The doctor said there's a good chance you'll recover," she reassured.

"How good?" I pressed, squeezing her hands as if they were a lifeline.

Flora's explanation brought a strange sense of relief, a glimmer of hope amidst the chaos. "You were hit hard on the back of your head," she explained gently, "and the injury was serious, discovered too late. There's a small blood clot pressing on your optic nerve. There are two possible ways to remove it: brain surgery or a non-invasive laser procedure."

I eased back into the bed, comforted somewhat by her words. "Colonel!" I called out, my voice steadying.

Colonel Jack's response was unexpected, his tone a mix of awkwardness and sincerity. "Forget it, no need to apologize. I don't blame you."

I retorted, "But I should blame you. Why did you leave me alone in Fludent Garden?"

There was a long silence, the only sound the faint sigh from Flora, who murmured, "Let's not dwell on it. It's done, and blaming anyone doesn't change things."

Colonel Jack's voice returned, seeking answers. "What happened in Fludent Garden? Who attacked you? The old servant has vanished, and Max Darcy claims he'll return soon. You need to tell me everything."

His insistence only fueled my frustration, my anger surging unchecked. "What do you care more about, Jack?" I burst out. "Is it the case details or the fact that I'm blind?"

Caught off guard, the colonel's voice wavered. "You don't have to be angry—"

But my patience snapped. "Get out! Leave!" I shouted, pointing blindly forward, aware of my finger trembling with emotion.

Colonel Jack seemed to chuckle bitterly, "Alright, I'll go. Calm down." He paused, adding with a touch of humor, "But I can't exit where you pointed—there's a wall there!"

If Flora hadn't been holding me down, I might have leaped up in indignation. Yet, as I heard the shuffle of departing footsteps, a sharp pain flared at the back of my head, pulling me back into the darkness.

Desperation clawed at me as my eyes strained against the void, seeking light and finding none. Flora's soothing voice wrapped around me, urging calmness. "You need rest. The doctor can't proceed until your head injury improves. Losing your temper won't help regain your sight."

I gripped her hand, feeling the medication's effects pulling me under, drifting into a restless sleep filled with vivid, chaotic dreams. In dreams, my sight returned, mocking my waking blindness. Upon waking, I pondered if those born blind dreamt, and what form their visions might take.

In the ensuing days, I drifted in and out of consciousness, with Flora ever-present. She informed me of Colonel Jack's repeated visits, his unspoken desire to converse, yet restrained by my condition.

The police continued their search for the "old servant," but I knew he had vanished, shedding his disguise and slipping away. I recounted to Jack how I discerned the servant's secret, but what use was it now?

My mind replayed the moment I turned and saw the peculiar metal tube in his hand. The tube was an enigma, a piece of advanced technology starkly out of place in the antiquated setting of Fludent Garden. Its presence suggested a deeper mystery beneath the surface.

What was being concealed? Only Max Darcy might hold the answers, yet he was miles away, despite my certainty of seeing him at the September Coffee House.

And the metal tube itself—where had it gone? I recalled falling upon it, the servant fleeing. If he hadn't returned, the police should have found it. Yet, Jack hadn't mentioned it.

Reaching out instinctively, I heard Flora's voice, "What are you looking for?"

"My things," I replied. "I wasn't wearing these clothes when brought here. Where are my belongings?"

"They're here," Flora assured, "I sorted them out and found something peculiar."

"A round metal tube?" I guessed.

"Yes," she confirmed, "I didn't know what it was but sensed its importance, so I secured it—and examined it."

I leaned in, anticipation rising, "What is it?"

Her response was a letdown, "I don't know. Its structure is intricate."

"At least, tell me what it resembles," I pressed. "The person aimed it at my back. What sort of device is it?"

Flora considered, "It resembles a camera, or something akin to it!"

Flora agreed to hide the metal tube, ensuring that no one else would know about its existence until I regained my eyesight. Just then, there was a knock at the door. Flora went to open it, and I instinctively called out, "Colonel, hello," recognizing the distinct sound of his leather shoes against the floor.

Colonel Jack seemed momentarily taken aback but soon spoke. "I just talked to the doctor. They mentioned your condition is improving."

I couldn't help but respond with a hint of irony. "That's like your routine answers to journalists, isn't it?"

He approached my bedside and hesitated before delivering news that set my heart racing. "Max Darcy is back from Penang."

This revelation unnerved me. The thought of facing Max Darcy, whom I believed to be the orchestrator of recent events, was daunting. In my usual state, I would relish the challenge of a formidable adversary. But now, as a blind man, the prospect was unsettling.

Colonel Jack continued, his words causing a sheen of sweat to form on my palms. "Max Darcy's first request upon arrival was to see you."

Despite my inner turmoil, I maintained a facade of calm. "Why would he want to see me? To apologize?"

Jack's tone was slightly exasperated. "I don't know. He came straight from the airport and is waiting outside. I think it must be important."

The colonel's inquiry nudged me toward a decision. Should I meet Max Darcy? Considering my current vulnerability, avoiding him wasn't an option.

"Okay, please let him in," I decided, bracing myself for the encounter.

I heard the colonel's footsteps, followed by the door opening and closing. Every nerve in my body tensed as Max Darcy approached. His voice, calm and measured, echoed the familiarity of our previous encounters. "I heard about your unfortunate situation from the colonel. I hope you recover soon."

Matching his composure, I replied, "Thank you for visiting."

The room fell silent, an unspoken tension hanging in the air until Colonel Jack broke it. "Mr. Darcy would like to speak with you alone. Are you agreeable to that?"

I had expected this request, knowing Max Darcy's visit had a purpose. Flora, however, interjected firmly, "No, he needs my care. I won't leave him."

I nodded in agreement, reinforcing her stance. "Yes, there are no secrets between my wife and me. If anyone should leave, it would be the colonel or Mr. Darcy

My stance was unmistakable—I would only engage in a discussion with Max Darcy if Flora remained by my side. If that condition was unacceptable to him, he was welcome to leave.

Silence enveloped the room, thick with tension and unspoken thoughts. I visualized Colonel Jack casting a questioning glance at Max Darcy, perhaps seeking his consent. Despite my reservations about their relationship, I didn't suspect any collusion. It seemed more likely that Jack was merely extending the courtesy due to Max Darcy's standing.

After a moment that felt interminable, Max Darcy acquiesced. "Alright, Colonel, please give us a moment alone," he finally said, his voice steady yet carrying an undercurrent of something I couldn't quite place—perhaps determination, perhaps resignation.

I imagined Colonel Jack's expression, caught between professional obligation and personal discomfort, as he exited the room, closing the door softly behind him. Now, with only Flora, Max Darcy, and myself present, the atmosphere shifted subtly, charged with anticipation.

Knowing the stakes, I initiated the conversation with a strategic opener. "Mr. Darcy, please speak freely. Everything you say to me, you say to my wife as well. We share everything."

Though not entirely true, I implied it to signal that any threat to me would also concern Flora. It was a strategic move, indicating that dealing with me meant dealing with us both.

Originally, I tackled all the strange experiences outside on my own, with occasional collaborations with Flora. But now, I need Flora's help because I can't see anything.

Flora must understand this, which is why she insists on staying by my side.

Max Darcy's deep breath was audible, a prelude to his measured response. "Mr. Morris, I understand your first visit was under the pretense of real estate, but truly about Mr. Bond's disappearance."

"Correct," I replied, matching his calmness. "The real estate inquiry was merely a cover."

His dry laughter followed, devoid of humor, more an acknowledgment of the complexity of the situation. "You've uncovered quite a bit, haven't you?"

I countered his insinuation with a knowing smile, "That depends on your perspective. By my standards, I've barely scratched the surface."

Acknowledging my point, Max Darcy continued, "At the very least, you recognize that all roads lead back to me."

"If I didn't, I wouldn't know anything at all," I remarked, my tone one of deliberate confidence.

With a few more chuckles, he posed the pivotal question, "What will it take for you to stop and let things remain as they are?"

His directness was a challenge, a demand for transparency that left little room for maneuver. But I was prepared. My reply was swift, likely catching him off guard with its clarity. "I need to know everything. Only then can I determine whether to proceed or desist."

This was a defining moment in our exchange, each of us scrutinizing the other's resolve, searching for any sign of weakness or intent. I knew that the path ahead would be fraught with challenges, but I was determined to see it through, with Flora at my side.

The room grew quiet again, and I imagined Colonel Jack seeking Max Darcy's approval. I wondered if there was any unspoken agreement between them, though I doubted they collaborated. Jack likely respected Darcy for his status.

Finally, Max Darcy conceded. "Okay, Colonel, please give us a moment."

I imagined Jack's reluctant departure, followed by the door closing once more. Now, it was just the three of us. I seized the opportunity to speak first. "Mr. Darcy, feel free to speak openly. My wife is aware of everything I know."

Though not entirely true, I implied it to signal that any threat to me would also concern Flora. It was a strategic move, indicating that dealing with me meant dealing with us both.

Max Darcy took a deep breath before speaking. "Mr. Morris, your initial visit was about Mr. Bond's disappearance, wasn't it?"

"Yes," I confirmed, "The real estate inquiry was just a pretense."

He chuckled dryly, a sound that suggested resignation rather than amusement. "Mr. Morris, you know quite a bit now, don't you?"

I retorted with a sneer, "That depends on your definition. By my standards, I know far too little."

Max Darcy acknowledged, "At least you understand that everything ties back to me."

"If I didn't know that," I laughed, "I wouldn't know anything at all!"

His laughter was brief, but he quickly shifted to a direct question. "What will it take for you to stop and leave me be?"

His inquiry was straightforward yet forceful, demanding an immediate display of intentions.

I responded without hesitation, likely surprising him with my assertiveness. "Tell me everything. Only then will I decide if I should stop."

The conversation was at a crucial juncture, each of us gauging the other's resolve.

I could sense Max Darcy's frustration, even though I couldn't see his face. His breathing quickened, betraying his anger and struggle to maintain control. I held my silence, waiting for his next move. After a tense pause, he finally spoke, his tone laced with an attempt at calm. "Everything you claim to know is not evidence. You know I wasn't even in the city."

"True," I conceded, "I haven't disclosed everything to the colonel, and you won't be seeing the inside of a courtroom. But make no mistake, I won't stop pursuing this. Even blind, I'm not giving up."

Max Darcy took another breath, seemingly regaining composure. "Mr. Morris," he addressed me, his tone shifting to a more measured, almost sorrowful cadence, "you can't understand what I'm doing. No one can. Mr. Bond's disappearance was purely accidental."

"And Rory's death?" I pressed.

"Even more unforeseen," he replied bitterly.

"What about Jude Bailey's disappearance?" I continued, my questions relentless.

Max Darcy offered no answer, so I raised my voice, demanding, "And my being targeted?"

Silence stretched, thick and heavy. I declared, "Mr. Darcy, you are a criminal. The law may not touch you yet, but I won't let this go."

I heard his knuckles crack, likely a reflexive response to my accusation. The tension in the room was palpable, and after a long pause, Flora intervened, her voice firm yet polite. "I'm sorry, Mr. Darcy. If you've finished, he needs to rest."

Max Darcy's silence was telling. I heard his footsteps, heavy with anger, retreat from the room.

Colonel Jack entered soon after, peppering me with questions that seemed trivial given the circumstances. My patience wore thin, and I dismissed him curtly. Once alone with Flora, she leaned close, whispering, "Since you spoke so frankly, I want to know everything."

I nodded, recounting the series of events and my deductions. Flora listened intently, absorbing each detail. When I finished, she reflected, "Max Darcy seemed desperate for your understanding, yet he left angry."

"Time will tell if he's the criminal I suspect," I said. "If someone comes after us, that will be confirmation. We must be vigilant."

Flora voiced her concern, aware of my vulnerability. "Should we ask Jack for more protection?"

I shook my head. "Better to deal with threats quietly than invite more scrutiny."

Flora didn't argue, simply held my hand, her presence a silent reassurance.

Surprisingly, the next few days passed without incident. Colonel Jack's visits dwindled, and I remained undisturbed at the hospital. The doctor assured me that my head injury was healing, and the blood clot would soon dissolve, restoring my sight.

Despite being confined to the ward, I kept busy. Colleagues from Steve Bond's office visited, and I continued to issue directives, though Steve Bond remained elusive and no more strange calls occurred. Similarly, there was no sign of Jude Bailey.

Monitoring Max Darcy continued, yet he remained secluded within Fludent Garden, his movements a mystery even to those observing him.

On the day of my scheduled laser procedure, I was tense, uncertain of the outcome. If successful, I would regain my sight; if not, what then?

As I was prepped for surgery and my head secured, I heard the doctors speaking in hushed tones, aware of the rarity of such procedures. At that moment, I felt like a guinea pig, caught in a labyrinth of circumstances beyond my control.

Under local anesthesia, I was blissfully unaware of the operation's details until, suddenly, light pierced my vision. Real light, not a dream.

I discerned a circular light overhead, and gradually, shapes materialized before me. The doctor's voice, laden with anticipation, instructed, "If you can see now, please close your eyes for a moment."

Their tension was evident, awaiting confirmation of the procedure's success. I should have complied instantly, signaling success and prompting celebration.

But as I prepared to shut my eyes, a thought struck with clarity: My vision was restored, but Max Darcy didn't know this. Could I leverage this unnoticed advantage?

Chapter 9

The Accomplice's Visit

If Max Darcy continued to believe I was blind, I could use this to my advantage. Rather than inform the hospital to keep my recovery a secret, I opted to feign blindness by not closing my eyes during the procedure.

Seeing the doctors' disappointment was difficult. They were genuinely invested in restoring my sight, and I felt guilty for deceiving them. One doctor suggested trying again, but the attending physician advised waiting three months to avoid potential harm to my brain.

I spoke up, weakly suggesting, "I'm willing to try again in three months."

The attending doctor, his face lined with concern, examined my eyes with an instrument. He couldn't detect my deceit, as my blindness was due to optic nerve pressure, not a structural issue.

Upon leaving the operating room, Flora approached, visibly upset by the "bad news." Her haggard appearance pained me, but I waited until late at night, when we were alone, to reveal the truth.

Stunned by my revelation, Flora eventually spoke, "I've never criticized your choices, but this is too harsh on the doctors who tried so hard to help you."

I offered a bitter smile, "I know, but I need this edge against Max Darcy. I'll be discharged tomorrow, and he'll assume I'm still blind."

Though Flora disagreed, she knew my mind was set. The following day, with the doctor's approval, I returned home. I continued to act as if I needed assistance, aware of the irony that, while I could see, others thought I couldn't. Despite my guilt, the situation was strangely intriguing.

Shortly after settling in, I received a phone call. Flora answered, then covered the receiver, whispering, "It's a strange voice."

Taking the phone, I heard labored breathing, followed by a rushed apology. "Mr. Morris, please forgive me. I didn't meant it. I just acted impulsively."

Recognizing the "old servant's" voice filled me with excitement. I replied sternly, "You'd better hide, or I'll make you regret it."

He was panting, "No, I need to see you!" This unexpected request caught me off guard.

In the current situation, it was somewhat unbelievable that the "old servant"—the very one who once attacked me and nearly blinded me for life—would voluntarily come to meet me.

Was there a conspiracy? His anxiety seemed genuine, but I remained cautious. Before I could respond, he pleaded, "I know I hurt you, but I have important things to tell you. You have to see me."

I paused, then responded slowly, "You're mistaken. I can't see you or anything else."

The phone line was silent except for a startled gasp. He insisted, "I deeply regret it, but I must speak to you."

After a moment's thought, I agreed, "Fine, if you must come, I'll be here. I can't leave, nor do I want to."

The "old servant" quickly agreed, "I'll come!"

Hanging up, I explained to Flora, "It's the man from Fludent Garden. His role in these events is as significant as Max Darcy's."

Concerned, Flora asked, "Is this a trap?"

I reassured her, "Regardless of his intent, it's an opportunity. Even if he hadn't come, I would seek him out."

Flora nodded, and I added, "I'll handle him alone."

She looked puzzled, so I explained, "Don't worry, I'm pretending to be blind. If he believes I can't see, he'll be less guarded, and I'll discern his intentions. Your presence might alert him."

Understanding, Flora agreed. She hid behind a screen, and I composed myself to appear convincingly blind.

Fifteen minutes later, the doorbell rang. I called out, "Come in, it's unlocked!"

The door opened, and someone entered. I didn't look up, maintaining the facade. Observing him could wait; convincing him of my blindness was paramount.

The young man stood hesitantly at the door, his foot pausing as if unsure whether to proceed. I lifted my head slightly, maintaining the guise of blindness, and said, "Why don't you come in?"

The "old servant" entered, closing the door behind him, and approached me. I felt a mix of emotions as I addressed him, "I shouldn't have to face you again. You caused me the greatest pain of my life."

Deliberately, I turned my head in the wrong direction, but with my eyes open, I could see him clearly. He was surprisingly young, perhaps 23 or 24, with a pale complexion and nervous hands constantly rubbing together. As I spoke, he wiped his sweaty palms on his clothes, stammering, "I-I—"

He seemed to struggle with finding the right words, perhaps intending to apologize but unsure how to proceed. I sighed, "Since you're here, have a seat. If you need a drink, help yourself. I'm not accustomed to the dark, and there's no one else here."

He sat across from me, his hands visibly trembling. He reached out, and I tensed, uncertain of his intentions. Yet, I remained composed, not flinching even as his hand neared me. It was a challenge, but I managed to appear unalarmed. His hand withdrew just before contact—perhaps a gesture of awkward comfort rather than malice.

We sat in silence until he finally murmured, "Mr. Morris, please forgive me. I was really startled at the time."

I frowned, touching the bandaged wound on my head, then dismissed his apology with a wave. "Let's move past that. You're here for a reason. What were you doing with that metal pipe? Why point it at me? Explain."

His unease was palpable, and he rubbed his hands nervously. "Mr. Morris, my name is Harry York."

His response was unrelated, seemingly evading my questions with insincerity. Yet, offering his name suggested he intended to start afresh. What was his plan? Although unfamiliar, the name sparked a memory. I recalled reading about him — a digital prodigy who entered university at sixteen and earned a doctorate by twenty.

Realizing who he was, I nodded. "Mr. York, are you the prodigy known as the comet of the mathematical world?"

Harry York's bitter smile confirmed it. "Yes, I've achieved much in mathematics, but I'm nothing compared to Mr. Darcy."

His words sent a jolt through me, and I almost forgot to maintain my facade of blindness. If Max Darcy was indeed the "Mr. Darcy" he referred to, then his true identity was astonishing. Dr. Ethan Darcy, a celebrated scientist praised even by Einstein, was rumored to be Max Darcy.

I addressed Harry York, "The Mr. Darcy you mean—is he Dr. Ethan Darcy?"

Harry nodded, and though I shouldn't have seen it, I pressed for verbal confirmation. "Is Max Darcy him?"

After a pause, Harry confirmed, "It's him."

I was momentarily speechless, then asked, "Why are two brilliant scientists like you hiding your identities? What are you doing?"

Dr. Harry's lips quivered. "We're conducting an experiment."

I scoffed, "Your actions resemble criminal activity more than scientific research!"

Dr. Harry flinched at my accusation, then explained, "We never intended this, but the research demands immense funding. It's money we can't raise in our lifetimes without support, and—and—"

His panic was evident as he looked around, fearing eavesdroppers. I pressed him, "And what?"

Voice wavering with emotion, Harry replied, "I — I shouldn't say. We vowed secrecy. I don't know if I should break that promise."

His hands twisted together anxiously. The room was silent, save for his labored breathing and the tension hanging in the air. Flora, hidden behind the screen, remained perfectly still, a testament to her composure.

I continued coldly, "You need to speak. Your cover's blown, and as a scientist, you owe it to your conscience. Don't resort to criminality to hide when exposed."

His forehead glistened with sweat, and I hoped my words would compel him to reveal the truth.

I had a strong sense that Dr. Harry's conscience was tormenting him, and with a little more pressure, he would reveal everything. I seized the opportunity, saying, "Mr. Bond's disappearance, Rory's death, and Jude Bailey's vanishing—are these all consequences of your attempts to hide your activities?"

Harry's hands trembled violently. "No, no, they were accidents, complete accidents!" His fists clenched, and his voice was filled with desperation.

I pressed further, "What exactly is your work?"

His lips quivered, but he remained silent, clearly battling an inner turmoil. Seeing this, I adopted a firmer tone. "You need to tell me everything. No more hesitations."

Harry stood, looking lost and conflicted. My stern gaze bore into him as he stammered, "I—I can't say. The people supporting our experiments—"

He stopped abruptly, and I lost my patience. "If you won't talk, then leave!" I ordered, pointing towards the door.

Harry backed away, nearly in tears. "Please, don't force me. If I talk, I'll be killed!"

I scoffed, "Then why are you here?"

With a pained expression, he confessed, "I came to ask for the return of the—camera."

I was momentarily taken aback, realizing he meant the metal pipe, which Flora had described as incredibly complex. His audacity to ask for it back was astonishing. I replied coldly, "No, I'll use it to expose your crimes."

Harry's voice grew desperate, "You won't defeat them. You can't see anything; you can't win against them. For your sake and mine, please, don't interfere. Leave it alone, and nothing will happen."

I laughed bitterly, "That's absurd. Mrs. Bond cries every day, waiting for her husband."

"Mr. Bond will return," Harry insisted, "If we calm down and correct our mistakes, he can come back."

His words were cryptic, and I couldn't resist asking, "Where is Mr. Bond?"

Harry covered his face, his voice a whisper, "Don't force me." With that, he turned, fled through the door, and slammed it shut. I heard his panicked breathing from the other side.

I opened the door, seeing Harry sprinting away like a frightened rabbit. Hesitating briefly, I watched as he darted into the street, just as a car screeched to a halt beside him.

Two burly men jumped out, grabbing Harry before he could escape.

It was a dilemma. If I intervened, my ruse of blindness would be blown. But if I stayed silent, Harry would be in real danger. My decision was swift; I shouted, "Mr. Harry, please come back! I have something to tell you!"

My cry could be interpreted as a blind man's attempt to reach out, maintaining my cover while potentially aiding Harry. But it was in vain. The men shoved him into the car, and one glanced back at me before they sped off, narrowly avoiding a collision with another vehicle. The driver of the near-miss car yelled angrily as they disappeared from sight.

I stood at the door, my heart pounding. The reason for my surprise was not Harry's kidnapping, but rather what he had confided in me. Harry claimed that a "behind the scenes host" was targeting both him and Max Darcy. If he divulged secrets about their research, this "host" would undoubtedly ensure his silence.

I hadn't had the chance to learn who the masterminds behind Harry and Max Darcy were. But just now, one of the two men who kidnapped Harry and got into the car turned around, and I saw his face clearly. That alone was enough to surprise me!

I recognized him—the man known as "Shark."

Standing at the door, my mind raced with the implications of what I had just witnessed. The sight of Shark, a notorious figure known for his control over a significant portion of the global drug market, personally involved in the abduction of Harry was shocking. Shark's presence suggested that the situation was far more serious than I had initially imagined.

Shark was a man of immense influence, typically operating through intermediaries to maintain his distance from direct criminal activities. His personal involvement meant that he was acting under the orders of someone even more powerful—a "behind-the-scenes host" with enough clout to compel Shark to act personally.

This revelation left me with more questions than answers. Who could wield such influence over a figure as formidable as Shark? Despite my extensive knowledge of global criminal networks, I struggled to identify anyone with the authority to direct Shark in this manner. The mastermind behind this operation was clearly a force to be reckoned with, someone operating at the highest echelons of power.

Lost in thought, I barely registered Flora's approach until she was standing behind me. I remained fixed in place, staring into the now-calm street. "Harry was taken," I said, my voice tinged with disbelief. "And one of the men who took him was Shark."

Flora, aware of Shark's reputation, was understandably shocked. "Are you sure? You might have mistaken him," she said, though I could tell she knew I was certain.

I turned to face her, my expression resolute. "I'm certain. His scar is unmistakable. If my guess is correct, Shark saw me too. He knows who I am, and there's a chance he might try to contact me."

Flora's reaction was a mix of concern and disgust. Her desire to distance herself from underworld figures like Shark was evident. Despite my attempts to reassure her, the gravity of the situation weighed heavily on both of us.

"Don't worry," I said, trying to inject some confidence into my voice. "Shark has worked hard to build a legitimate facade. He won't jeopardize that lightly. If he approaches me, it'll be discreet, likely to dissuade me from digging any deeper."

Flora nodded but remained silent, her thoughts clearly troubled. We moved inside, and I closed the door, mulling over my next steps.

The metal pipe — Harry's "camera" — was the only tangible clue I had, and I resolved to examine it further, hoping it might reveal more about the mysterious experiment and the shadowy figure orchestrating these events.

As I methodically disassembled the device, I contemplated the precarious path I was on. The stakes were higher than ever, with powerful adversaries lurking in the shadows. Yet, armed with determination and a growing understanding of the forces at play, I felt ready to confront whatever challenges awaited.

Chapter 10

Fortune's Bribe

As I examined the peculiar device, I pondered Harry's claim that it was a camera. It certainly didn't resemble any camera I was familiar with. One end featured a convex glass component, reminiscent of a lens, yet unlike any lens I'd seen before. Inside the metal tube was a complex array of radio controls and integrated circuits, akin to a microcomputer, which was quite advanced for its time.

Spending an entire hour meticulously disassembling and reassembling the device, I documented every step. It was crucial to capture these details, considering that Harry—and by extension, the "behind-the-scenes host"—was keen on retrieving it. Initially, I hadn't fully appreciated the gravity of the situation, but after encountering Shark, I realized the stakes were higher than I'd imagined.

Anticipating that I might be coerced into relinquishing this evidence, I took numerous photographs, intending to consult experts who could shed light on its true purpose. Understanding the device's function could provide valuable insights into the broader mystery.

As I completed my analysis, dusk settled in. Suddenly, I heard the sound of several cars arriving. Peering out the window, I saw three large RVs parked outside. Two men approached my door, one of whom I recognized as Shark. The other, larger man carried a substantial crocodile leather bag.

I listened from the study door as Flora addressed them. "I'm sorry, Mr. Morris is not in the mood for visitors today."

Shark's voice, gruff yet insistent, responded, "Mrs. Morris, I've already spoken with him today. My name is Syed, and I assure you, I mean no harm."

I stepped into the stairwell and called out, "Who insists on seeing me?"

Feigning blindness, I descended slowly, gripping the banister. Shark's voice reached up to me, "It's me, Mr. Morris, Shark!"

When I reached the bottom, I saw Flora still standing at the door, blocking Shark and his men.

Of course, I had to avoid any hint of premonition of his arrival, so when I stood still, with an extremely puzzled expression, I asked, "Shark? Aren't you that—"

Before I could finish speaking, he interrupted, "I am that Shark, Mr. Morris!"

I stretched my hands forward and said, "Please come in!"

As I sat across from Shark, I couldn't help but contemplate the strange turn of events that had brought us face to face. A notorious figure like Shark was the last person I expected to find myself conversing with, especially given the enigmatic research involving Max Darcy and Harry York. The intersection of a renowned scientist with a criminal overlord was baffling, hinting at deeper, undisclosed connections.

Shark broke the silence, acknowledging my reputation with a chuckle, "Mr. Morris, I've heard of you for quite some time. You've been quite the thorn for many acquaintances of mine."

I returned his smile with a faint one of my own, recognizing his attempt to steer the conversation.

But I was under no illusions—this was no social call. "Let's get to the point," I said evenly. "I can't imagine what would warrant a meeting between us."

Shark responded with a philosopher's drawl, "Don't say that. Opportunities for connections arise in the most unexpected ways. Mr. Morris, there's a task requiring utmost discretion. I want you to oversee security for it."

His proposition caught me off guard, and I struggled to grasp its full meaning. "I'm sorry—" I began, letting the implication hang in the air. My reluctance was clear; I had no interest in aligning myself with criminal endeavors.

Shark, perceptive as ever, caught on instantly. "Don't worry, Mr. Morris. This isn't my usual line of work. I've been asked to assist, and while I was initially managing security, it seems I'm not suited for it. That's why I'm recommending you."

Realization dawned on me. This task likely involved the research project of Max Darcy and Harry York. Despite my suspicions, I maintained my facade of ignorance. "Mr. Syed, if you can't handle it, I doubt I could. Besides, as you can see, I've lost my sight and am quite limited in what I can do."

Shark made a series of noises, difficult to interpret but suggestive of amusement or exasperation. "You're too modest. This role requires little more than your mental acuity."

He paused, gauging my reaction, and continued, "I assure you—though perhaps my assurances mean little—this is no criminal enterprise. It's entirely legitimate."

Feigning mild curiosity, I replied, "Your secrecy is intriguing. What is this all about?"

I knew I was treading on thin ice, balancing between feigned interest and genuine curiosity. Shark's demeanor suggested he believed in the legitimacy of the task, or at least wanted me to believe it. But the involvement of figures like him hinted at complexities and risks far beyond the surface, and I needed to remain vigilant.

Shark seemed to struggle with his words before finally explaining,"It's simple. A great scientist has a project—though I don't understand the science of it—and he needs a highly confidential environment for his research. He wants you to help with that confidentiality." Shark had laid his cards on the table. Pretending ignorance would only confirm his suspicions, so I decided to engage more openly.

I chuckled, "Mr. Syed, you're truly clever. Instead of asking me to keep a secret, you're asking me to protect it."

Shark laughed in return, "You've already guessed what it's about. Harry York stopped by, didn't he?"

"Yes," I replied, "but he was too nervous to say much and left quickly."

Shark acknowledged Harry's cautiousness, then shifted the conversation, "Mr. Morris, if you accept this position, here's your fee."

Shark reached out and took a crocodile leather bag from one of his henchmen, placed it on the table, unzipped it, and opened the bag. I immediately saw that it was full of hundred-dollar bills, and for a moment, I couldn't estimate how many there were. As the bag was opened, Shark stared at me closely, clearly wondering if I was truly blind. He had his doubts. Otherwise, he wouldn't have taken the opportunity to observe my reaction.

But Shark found nothing in my expression. He naturally thought that ordinary people would react strangely when seeing so many banknotes at once.

Shark's attempt to intimidate me with the sight of a bag full of U.S. dollars was a calculated move to test my resolve and the authenticity of my blindness. However, his effort was wasted; my past experiences had exposed me to significant wealth, allowing me to maintain an air of calm and indifference. His voice was firm, "Look!"

"I can't see it," I replied evenly, reinforcing my facade.

He grabbed a handful of cash and placed it in my hand. I felt the crisp bills, acknowledging, "It's money, U.S. dollars?" He confirmed, "Yes, two million in total. It's yours if you agree."

I let the money slip through my fingers and fall to the ground, unimpressed. "Such a high price for my cooperation is quite shocking, Mr. Syed."

Shark's eyes narrowed as he said, "If we spend so much and gain nothing, that would indeed be shocking."

I pressed him, "You promised this has nothing to do with crime, yet people have disappeared, and one has died mysteriously. How do you explain that?"

Caught off guard, Shark hesitated before responding, "As I said, I don't understand the science. They claim it was an accident, not deliberate."

I challenged him further, "I've heard that excuse too often. What kind of accident causes death and disappearance?"

His silence was telling, his expression darkening. "You could make me the victim of another 'accident,' saving your money," I suggested.

Shark's demeanor shifted, becoming more menacing. "The people funding this don't care about money. If you oppose us, what you suggest isn't impossible."

His threat hung in the air, but I met it with a cold smile, "I'll await that outcome, then."

Shark rose, visibly angry, yet halted before leaving. "Why? You've already paid a great price, losing your sight."

"Exactly," I replied, "and now I need compensation."

He kicked the coffee table in frustration, "This money is your compensation!"

I sighed, "Mr. Syed, you misunderstand. I don't want money. My needs are met. What I desire is the truth—the return of Mr. Bond and Jude Bailey, and understanding the cause of Rory's death."

Shark's breathing quickened, a mix of anger and apprehension. "You won't find answers," he shouted.

"I'm willing to try," I said firmly.

Flora, calm and composed, gathered the money, placing it back in the bag. "Mr. Syed, he needs rest. Please leave," she said.

Shark glared at her, but her poise seemed to unsettle him. He picked up the bag, offering it one last time, "I'll buy that device from you."

I declined, "Dr. Harry calls it a camera, worth as much as those used by astronauts. But it's not for sale."

Shark, losing patience, barked, "You've no use for it!"

I maintained my calm, "Someone values it highly enough to offer this much money."

Shark, seething with anger, stormed towards the door, pausing to issue a final warning. "Ash Morris, you live up to your reputation, but persistence won't benefit you."

I retorted, "I've faced threats all my life."

He turned, his face a mask of fury, "I'm not threatening, just stating facts. There's no crime here, nothing of interest to you."

Raising my voice, I pressed, "A friend vanished without cause. Is that your handiwork?"

Shark, visibly irate, denied involvement, "If it were my doing, I'd be a scientist!"

His words struck me, adding a layer of complexity. His denial suggested the disappearances were linked to the scientists, Max Darcy and Flora. But why would scientists cause such events? The mystery deepened, and I knew uncovering the truth would require navigating a web of secrets and powerful players.

As Shark's men opened the door and he prepared to leave, I realized I had to pivot my approach if I hoped to unravel the mystery at hand. "Please wait a moment," I called out.

Shark paused, not turning back. "You mentioned you were sent by someone," I probed.

His response was cold and dismissive, "Yes, but I won't reveal who."

I didn't expect him to, knowing that the person behind him was likely the elusive "behind-the-scenes host" Flora had alluded to. "It seems your patron made a mistake by sending you," I suggested lightly, trying to pique his interest.

Though Shark's back was to me, I sensed his irritation. It wasn't my intention to provoke him, so I quickly added, "There's nothing to resolve between us. Perhaps Max Darcy or Flora should visit me instead."

Shark turned, scrutinizing me. After a tense pause, he asked, "If they come, will you drop this matter?"

"I can't promise that," I admitted, "but there's room for negotiation. I trust their words more."

He considered this, then nodded. "Alright, I can arrange a meeting. You're a clever man."

I gave a genuine, albeit weary, smile. "I'd rather be a fool in this situation."

Shark hefted the briefcase, hesitated as if to say more, then departed with his entourage. Flora closed the door, leaning against it, "What do you think?"

I pondered silently before responding, "I hope he'll arrange for me to meet Max Darcy."

Flora shook her head, "I'm more curious about the 'mastermind' behind all this."

I couldn't offer an answer, so I turned the question back to her, "Any thoughts?"

"This person must be significant. If we heard their name, we'd likely recognize it," Flora speculated.

I nodded in agreement, "That's likely."

"And," Flora continued, "they're probably in league with criminal elements."

I considered this, "You base that on Shark's involvement? While he's a gangster, his connections are vast. Even small nations rely on him for arms."

Flora sighed and was about to walk forward when the doorbell suddenly rang. She immediately turned around and opened the door.

As soon as the door opened, I forgot to conceal my surprised expression. This was truly unexpected. Shark had only left less than three minutes ago, and now standing at the door was Max Darcy!

Max Darcy stood there, his previous appearances flashing through my mind. Each time we had seen him, he wore different costumes, indicating he had never undergone makeup.

His expression was filled with anger and nervousness, but he was trying his best to suppress his emotions. "I hear someone wants to speak with me directly," he announced.

Flora, recognizing him despite their lack of introduction, invited him in, "Mr. Darcy? Please, come in."

Max Darcy entered briskly, his anger palpable. As he approached, he demanded, "Why are there so many meddlers in the world?"

Suppressing my irritation, I replied, "Mr. Darcy, a friend has disappeared, and I've lost my sight. This isn't meddling, wouldn't you agree?"

His retort was sharp, "Your friend will return if you stop interfering. As for your blindness, you might fool others, but not me!"

His revelation that my blindness was a sham took me aback. How had he discerned the truth so quickly?

Momentarily stunned, I stood there, unsure of how to respond.

Max Darcy, detecting my unease, sneered and took a seat. I managed to collect myself, waving off the awkwardness as I sat opposite him.

"You have nothing to gain, so why make this difficult?" Max Darcy challenged. "Is your curiosity so insatiable that you'd jeopardize a grand vision?"

His exposure of my ruse left little room for denial, so I abandoned the charade. "Mr. Darcy, your acumen extends beyond science," I acknowledged, impressed.

In this unexpected encounter, I realized the stakes were higher than I had considered. Max Darcy's involvement and the enigmatic forces at play suggested a complex web of ambitions and secrets. Uncovering the truth would require careful navigation and a willingness to confront the unknown.

Max Darcy's confidence was palpable, and his demeanor suggested that he believed he was in the right. "Blindness is a significant change," he explained, "and maintaining one's original position in such circumstances is nearly impossible."

I nodded, acknowledging his point. "True, but Mr. Darcy, this isn't just about curiosity. You're an esteemed scientist, yet it's clear that a mysterious figure controls your actions."

His defense was swift and firm. "I volunteer for this. My work requires funding beyond what you can imagine. Without it, I can't proceed."

"So that includes owning a multi-story building?" I probed.

Max Darcy admitted candidly, "Yes!"

I pressed on, "What's the building's purpose? An investment, or something else?"

The mention of the building seemed to catch him off guard, though I wasn't sure why I'd fixated on it. Perhaps it was instinct, sensing something unusual about it.

Max Darcy hesitated, then conceded, "Mr. Morris, you are indeed perceptive."

I wasn't entirely sure what he meant, but I seized the moment. "Everything peculiar began with that building."

He fell silent, contemplating my words. His anger subsided, replaced by resignation. "What will it take for you to stop?"

He is negotiating terms with me. In any case, if the other party takes the initiative to negotiate terms with you, you may as well ask for a sky-high price. This is an unchanging iron law! Recognizing an opportunity, I leaned back, then forward, speaking deliberately, "I want to know the entire truth."

Max Darcy recoiled, "Impossible!"

I remained calm, "Once I know the truth, I can decide if it's worth keeping secret."

"You should know that even if you keep interfering, it won't cause any damage to my work.","" he insisted.

"That's what you think," I countered. "I have a plan, and I'm executing it."

"What plan?" he demanded, visibly anxious.

"I've contacted top scientific minds. I'm prepared to announce that you're conducting clandestine research. It'll be global news."

His face darkened, the threat of exposure clearly affecting him. I pressed further, "I've also spoken with Colonel Jack, who will initiate a thorough investigation into your backers."

Max Darcy's expression faltered, and I knew I had the upper hand. I leaned back, adopting a casual posture, "Consider your options."

In that moment, I caught a fleeting, malevolent gleam in his eye. Though it unsettled me, I dismissed it, confident in my position. This was my negligence, which had made it almost impossible for me to be with the familiar and lovely world any more.

Max Darcy thought for a while, then lowered his head, looking dejected. His expression strengthened my confidence, making me think he had been completely defeated. Of course, I no longer considered what the look in his eyes just now meant!

After a pause, Max Darcy offered, his head bowed. "If I arrange a meeting with Mr. Bond for you, will you come?"

His proposal was unexpected. I asked warily, "Why not bring Mr. Bond here?"

Max Darcy looked up, a resigned smile on his lips. "Some things are beyond our control, but I promise you can meet him."

Flora shook her head, cautioning against trust, but the offer was too enticing. Despite her warning, I agreed, "Alright, take me to him."

Max Darcy nodded, and I rose to join him. He glanced at Flora, who immediately declared, "I'm coming too!"

As we prepared to leave, I sensed the gravity of my decision. The prospect of meeting Mr. Bond was compelling, yet the risks were undeniable. With Flora by my side, I felt a measure of reassurance, ready to face whatever lay ahead in pursuit of the truth.

Chapter 11

Odd Occurrences Resurface

Max Darcy shook his head, his voice carrying an air of inevitable finality. "I'm sorry, but only Mr. Morris can come with me."

Flora shot me a knowing glance—a silent communication of doubt. My confidence, perhaps, bordered on hubris. It seemed likely that Max Darcy had Steve Bond hidden away somewhere. The prospect of accompanying him alone was fraught with danger, but nothing ventured, nothing gained. The pull of discovery was stronger.

I turned to Flora, my resolve firm. "It's fine. I have to see Steve Bond."

Lowering her voice to a conspiratorial whisper, Flora said, "I have a feeling nothing has ever been as strange as this."

As she spoke, Max Darcy drifted to the paintings on the wall, feigning interest. It was a transparent attempt to give us privacy, though I doubted he truly cared for art in such a charged moment.

Flora's instincts couldn't be dismissed as mere intuition; the situation was bizarre and unsettling.

"Do you think I'm in danger?" I asked.

She squeezed my hand, her smile tinged with worry. "I can't say for sure, but Steve Bond's disappearance is a mystery. Now you're going to him—"

Her words hung in the air, unfinished, and I felt a flicker of hesitation. Where exactly was Steve Bond? Known for his resilience, his absence was troubling, hinting at forces beyond his considerable abilities.

Max Darcy offered to take me to see Steve Bond, a proposition that carried the implicit risk of sharing his fate. The question loomed—did I possess the means to escape the clutches of whatever power had ensnared him?

I lingered in thought before deciding, "Steve Bond is at the heart of this. I can't pass up the chance to see him."

Flora's brow furrowed, and with unexpected boldness, she called out, "Mr. Darcy, why can't I come too?"

Max Darcy turned, his hands a picture of helplessness. "I merely point the way. I can't go myself."

"Where is it?" she pressed.

His reply was maddeningly vague. "I don't know, I don't know!"

Frustration bubbled up. "Are you joking?"

"No," he replied, shaking his head. "You might see Mr. Bond, and perhaps Mr. Bailey as well."

I was at a loss, faced with Max Darcy's enigmatic demeanor. His helplessness deepened with a sigh. "Honestly, there's no guarantee you'll return."

Flora and I exchanged startled glances. Max Darcy's admission was chilling, yet his transparency suggested sincerity rather than malice. What, then, was the nature of this place?

Silence stretched between us, the room steeped in quiet tension. Finally, Flora spoke, her calm voice cutting through the stillness. "If such a strange place exists, you should visit it, even if returning is uncertain."

Her words resonated with my innate curiosity. Max Darcy's cryptic warning only intensified my determination to uncover the truth.

Resolute, I declared, "Give me a few minutes, and I'll join you."

Surprise flickered across Max Darcy's face. I gestured to Flora, and we ascended the stairs together.

In the study, I retrieved a small radio, testing its weight in my hand before pocketing it. "I'll stay in touch," I assured Flora.

She nodded, understanding the silent promise of communication. With a final nod to Flora, I rejoined Max Darcy downstairs, tapping his shoulder. "Let's go."

Flora followed us to the door, her wave a silent testament to her composure. Few could maintain such poise when a loved one ventured into the unknown.

Max Darcy led me outside, his offer casual yet loaded with implication. "Shall we take my car?"

With the radio tucked securely in my pocket, I felt a thin thread of connection back to Flora, confident that within the confines of the city, we wouldn't exceed its range. So, when Max Darcy suggested taking his car, I agreed without hesitation.

We drove in silence, the cityscape unfolding around us like a well-rehearsed play. As we ascended a familiar slope, déjà vu tugged at my consciousness. This incline was unmistakable—leading directly to that enigmatic building. The very building Steve Bond had shown me, where inexplicable events seemed to orbit. Why here? Had Steve Bond and Jude Bailey never left? Questions multiplied faster than answers, and before I could voice them, we were parked at the building's entrance.

"Please, step out," Max Darcy instructed, already exiting the vehicle. I followed, and we entered the building's lobby, enveloped in an unsettling stillness. The air was thick with an intangible weight, reminiscent of the day Rory had met his mysterious end on the rooftop. A chill crept up my spine as I questioned, "Why here? Is Steve Bond inside?"

Max Darcy's reply was a cryptic, infuriating, "Maybe."

Frustration prickled my skin. "What do you mean by that?"

The silence in the building was profound, hinting at our isolation. I braced for the possibility of an ambush, yet the quiet persisted. Max Darcy gestured towards the elevator. "You'll understand soon. You must go alone."

"Which way?" I demanded, suspicion sharpening my senses.

He pressed the elevator button, the doors sliding open with a soft chime. "This way," he said.

A realization struck me like a lightning bolt. The elevator. All peculiar events traced back to this very mechanism. Jude Bailey had vanished here, Steve Bond too, and now it was my turn to step into the unknown.

Apprehension rooted my feet to the floor, my gaze fixed on the elevator's maw. Max Darcy watched, a pained smile etched across his features. "I don't insist you go. But without seeing for yourself, you'll never grasp the truth."

His words dangled before me, a tantalizing lure. What truth lay shrouded in mystery, waiting beyond the confines of the elevator? "If you don't want to go," he urged, "let it go. But please, stop pursuing me."

His attempt to manipulate my resolve was transparent, yet effective. "Who said I wouldn't go?" I retorted, stepping decisively into the elevator. The doors sealed behind me with a mechanical whisper, and Max Darcy's voice filtered through the closing gap, "Remember what you see. I hope you return."

His anxious expression lingered in my mind as the elevator began its ascent. I glanced at the control panel—dark, devoid of the reassuring glow of numbered floors. The memories of Jude Bailey's account washed over me, beads of sweat collecting on my palms.

I'd ridden this elevator before, yet now, stripped of the familiar indicators, the journey felt alien. It ascended with a mechanical rhythm, surpassing the time it should have taken to reach the top. The reality of Jude Bailey's narrative unfolded around me, as the elevator climbed higher and higher, defying logic and architecture.

Five minutes passed; an eternity in elevator time. No structure could be this tall. Panic nipped at my mind, a primal instinct clawing at the constraints of reason. I yelled into the silence, the sound bouncing back at me—a solitary voice in a metal box.

Minutes dragged on, the ascent unyielding. "Max Darcy, where are you taking me?" I shouted, the query swallowed by the oppressive quiet. No response came, only the ceaseless ascent.

Fear's icy fingers tightened their grip, yet I clung to the recollection that Jude Bailey and Steve Bond had survived this harrowing ride. Perhaps, I reassured myself, I too would emerge unscathed, the mystery dispelled rather than deepened. But in those moments, suspended between floors and fate, the comforting whispers of logic were drowned by the roar of the unknown.

As I began to calm down, the elevator continued its seemingly endless ascent. It had been at least fifteen minutes, a surreal stretch of time in which I found myself alone in this iron cage. My mind raced, grappling with the absurdity of the situation: an elevator that never stopped, in a building devoid of life, with only me as its captive.

I pounded on the elevator doors, desperation lacing each thud, but the ascent persisted. The familiar yet now terrifying realization dawned upon me—this elevator, a simple contraption I relied on daily, had become a vessel of dread.

Driven by a mix of instinct and futility, I unscrewed a few panels with a knife, perhaps hoping for a mechanical deus ex machina to halt this maddening rise. As the aluminum plate clattered to the floor, I was met with an intricate web of circuits behind it. Layers upon layers of printed circuits, so complex that they could rival the innards of a supercomputer. Yet, here they were, hidden within an elevator.

This revelation shook me; elevators didn't require such elaborate machinery. But if it wasn't an elevator, then what was it? And more pressingly, what was it doing to me?

As I surveyed the labyrinth of technology, my knife brushed against a bundle of wires, and sparks flew, the air crackling with static. The machine was alive, operating with a purpose beyond my understanding.

Suddenly, the ascent ceased, the silence as abrupt as the halt. I turned to the elevator doors, which opened to reveal the hallway—familiar and yet surreal. I stumbled out, grateful for the solidity of the building, as if reuniting with an old friend after a long, harrowing journey.

Leaning against the wall, I caught my breath, wondering why I felt such fear. Despite the elevator's bizarre behavior, I remained within the building. What was there to fear?

Max Darcy had implied I'd see Steve Bond here. But if Steve Bond had been here all along, why hadn't he left?

Steeling myself for whatever lay ahead, I called into the silence, "If anyone is here, show yourself!"

As soon as I spoke, I heard a "clap" sound and a door slowly began to open. It creaked open at a deliberate pace, as if in a horror movie, where a mysterious character is about to emerge!

I stared intently as the door finally revealed its secrets. Standing there, staring back at me, was Jude Bailey!

Seeing Jude Bailey was unexpected and caught me off guard. For a moment, I was at a loss for words. His face was deathly pale and eerily terrifying.

His lips quivered, but for the first half-minute, he made no sound. It wasn't until later that he murmured, "You're here too...", his voice a whisper of disbelief.

Before I could respond, another door clicked open behind me. I turned to find Steve Bond standing there, his expression a mirror of Jude Bailey's—a mix of confusion and resignation. Relief flooded through me at the sight of him, and I rushed to his side, bombarding him with questions. "Steve Bond, what's happening? Why haven't you gone home?"

His response was a bitter smile, devoid of answers. "Come and see," he said, leading me inside. His movements were mechanical, as if guided by an unseen force.

I followed him, my curiosity piqued, expecting a revelation. But the room was unremarkable, an ordinary apartment devoid of anything extraordinary. "What am I supposed to see?" I asked, frustration tinging my words.

Steve Bond, now crouched in a corner, pointed towards the glass door leading to the balcony. Though his silence was unnerving, his gesture was clear.

I hesitated, doubts gnawing at me. From here, the balcony appeared mundane. Yet, as I stepped outside, reality shifted.

The cityscape, a familiar tableau of bustling life, was absent. In its place was a vast, unending void. No buildings, no streets, just an emptiness that swallowed all detail, leaving only the stark expanse of nothingness.

A chill raced down my spine, an instinctual fear gripping me. This was the void Jude Bailey had spoken of, a concept that seemed abstract until faced with its tangible presence.

Turning back, I saw Steve Bond still huddled in the corner. I returned inside, urgency lending strength to my voice. "Steve Bond, what is this? Where are we?"

Chapter 12

In Another Space

Steve Bond looked up at me, his eyes reflecting a mix of despair and bewilderment. "I don't know. I truly don't know."

The weight of his words settled heavily. I felt an urgency to break free from this unsettling place. "Let's go," I urged. "We'll figure it out once we're out."

Yet Steve Bond's expression turned even more sorrowful. "It's no use. It's impossible to leave here."

His response caught me off guard. "What do you mean? Is someone keeping you here?"

He shook his head. "No. I was alone at first. Then the administrator, Rory, appeared and disappeared again. Then Jude Bailey came, and now you."

His words were a jumble of confusion, so I pressed, "If Rory could leave, why can't we?"

Steve Bond's eyes met mine, filled with a deep-seated fear. "Rory jumped off the balcony. I don't have that kind of courage."

The revelation hit me like a cold wind. Rory's death had been a mystery, supposedly a fall from a high altitude—but from the balcony? It defied logic.

I stood there, momentarily lost for words, grappling with the surreal implications. After a pause, I asked, "Have you tried leaving by the stairs?"

He nodded, his voice dropping to a whisper. "Endless stairs. No matter how far you go, they just keep going. I tried everything."

As he spoke, his voice sharpened with urgency and fear. "We're in another world!"

The assertion was jarring. I approached Steve Bond, placing a steadying hand on his shoulder. "What do you mean by that?"

His breathing quickened, like a runner on the edge of collapse, and he repeated, "We're in another world."

I struggled to find words that might soothe him when the door creaked open, and Jude Bailey entered, pale and spectral. His presence only added to the otherworldly atmosphere. "Jude Bailey," I called, but he remained silent, eyes vacant.

Turning back to Steve Bond, I pressed him for answers, "You made a call once. What happened?"

His lips trembled as he searched for the words. "I don't know," he finally admitted.

Frustration flared. "You made the call! You must remember something!"

Steve Bond offered a bitter smile. "It was one of my many attempts to escape. I ran down the stairs, endlessly. It was like a nightmare. The stairs never ended."

He paused, gathering his thoughts, then continued. "I reached the second-floor management office. I thought there was hope. But no matter how long I ran, it was just stairs, more stairs."

His breath came in ragged gasps, the memory clearly taking its toll. I waited, not wanting to push him further.

"I remembered the phone on the second floor," Steve Bond said. "I didn't want to leave. I just wanted to call. I ran back up, saw the office again, and fought my way to the phone. I made a call. That's what happened."

Stunned, I recalled the recordings of his call—his voice distorted, slow, like a record played at the wrong speed. We had assumed it was a trick, a pre-recorded message altered somehow. But hearing him now, it seemed far more complex.

"And did you talk to her?" I asked.

Steve Bond nodded, his voice hollow. "Yes, I heard her voice. But it was sharp and fast, like a tape sped up, like a duck quacking."

A shiver ran down my spine. "And your voice was slowed down."

Steve Bond clutched his head, despairing. "Why is this happening? Why? Are we truly in another world?"

The question lingered in the air, heavy and unanswered. Here, in this uncanny space where reality seemed to bend and twist, the lines between worlds blurred, leaving us adrift in its wake.

In the dim glow of flickering fluorescent lights, Steve Bond muttered "in another world" like a mantra, his voice weaving a tapestry of mystery that seemed to hang in the air around him. As a newcomer to this strange setting, I couldn't quite grasp the gravity of his words. They danced on the periphery of my understanding, elusive and enigmatic.

Then, with the suddenness of a specter materializing from the shadows, Jude Bailey spoke. His voice sliced through the silence with an unexpected clarity: "Not another world, but another space."

The statement jolted me, a seismic shift in my perception, and Steve Bond's head snapped up, eyes wide with a mixture of surprise and revelation. It was clear from his reaction that this was the first time Jude Bailey had shared such a notion.

As the initial shock ebbed, curiosity surged to fill the void. "Mr. Bailey, what does 'another space' mean?" I asked, with a voice that barely concealed my intrigue.

Jude Bailey's bitter smile seemed to echo a thousand unspoken complexities. "I'm no scientist," he admitted, "but Max Darcy mentioned it. Another space, he said."

I forced myself into a semblance of calm, aware that any rashness might shatter the fragile thread of disclosure. Jude Bailey had always been the enigmatic figure at the heart of this labyrinth, and I suspected he concealed layers of secrets beneath his reticent exterior. Secrets that, if unveiled earlier, might have averted the chaos we now faced.

With a calculated pause, I addressed him: "Mr. Bailey, we're in this together now. Our fates are intertwined, for better or worse. It's time to lay everything bare."

In response, Jude Bailey's expression was a twisted blend of resignation and defiance. He turned away, colliding his forehead against the wall in a rhythmic, almost ritualistic display of frustration.

Steve Bond and I exchanged a silent pact of patience, allowing Jude Bailey the space he needed. Finally, he spun around, a decision reached. "Fine, I'll tell you. They've wronged me, after all."

As he began to unravel his tale, Steve Bond and I leaned in, our attention tethered to his every word. "I was the first to experience the oddities within the elevator," Jude Bailey confessed, recounting a brush with death and a subsequent hospital stay interrupted by a call from Max Darcy.

While his words were new, their essence was not; I had long suspected a clandestine link between him and Max Darcy.

"Mr. Darcy asked what I'd told the police," Jude Bailey continued, "and assured me my story would be dismissed as fantasy. He wanted to meet, and once I was discharged, I obliged."

Steve Bond and I remained silent, absorbing his narrative.

"Upon seeing me, Max Darcy handed me a hundred thousand yuan," Jude Bailey said, "to keep quiet. I agreed, but suspicion gnawed at me. If he could easily part with such a sum, what else might he be willing to offer?"

I interrupted with a sardonic laugh, unable to suppress my skepticism. "I didn't peg you for someone so avaricious."

Jude Bailey's smile was a weary acknowledgment of truth. "I demanded more, and each time, he paid. I even trailed him to his suburban abode, meeting him repeatedly. Every encounter was marked by hush money."

The story unfolded like a tightly wound coil slowly unraveling. "I proposed a final payoff for my silence. He claimed the funds came from others, but hinted at his research - a venture into realms beyond perception."

Steve Bond and I tensed, our imaginations ignited by the implications.

"He blamed me for my insatiable greed, insisting his work was revolutionary, not criminal. He said he wants to bring people into another space where they can freely control themselves, and that he's on the verge of success. He also mentioned that my entry into another space in the elevator was due to some uncontrollable technical issues. That's what he said."

We exchanged glances, grappling with the enormity of his revelation. The concept of "another space" defied comprehension, a challenge to our three-dimensional understanding of existence.

Steve Bond, breaking the silence, asked, "How did you end up here?"

Jude Bailey's laughter was laced with irony. "Max Darcy agreed to the payoff, but asked for my participation in one last experiment. He wanted me to enter the elevator, promising it was a gateway to that other space."

I exclaimed, "The elevator—a machine that manipulates dimensions!"

Jude Bailey nodded. "I consented, thinking it was a harmless test. But once inside, the path to return vanished."

His story concluded, I turned to Steve Bond, "What about you?"

He recounted his own strange journey: That night, I drove straight to the seaside, my mind a whirlwind of confusion. Leaving the car, I strolled along the coast, hoping to clear my thoughts. Suddenly, someone attacked me, knocking me unconscious. When I woke up, I was already in the elevator. As it came to a halt, I stepped out and found myself here. Since then, I've been here,"

I asked, "It's been many days, what do you rely on for a living?"

Steve Bond waved his hand dismissively. "It's strange. All my feelings seem to have stopped. I don't feel hungry, nor do I feel cold or hot. That's why I said I'm in another world!"

I was extremely confused. Although Jude Bailey had already revealed his secret, it didn't help much with the situation.

I learned that in this other space, everything was brought in by Max Darcy, and the tool he used to bring us here was the elevator in that building—an extraordinary and complex machine.

Max Darcy repeatedly claimed that everything was caused by technical errors, not intentional actions. Moreover, he stated that his research wasn't yet at a mature stage.

In other words, he could use the machine to send us into another space, but he didn't have the power to bring us back to our original world.

In the labyrinthine corridors of thought where reality often bends and curves, I finally grasped the gravity of his cryptic invitation for me to meet Steve Bond. His words had been a siren's warning: returning might be forever beyond my reach.

Back then, no permutation of my imagination could have conjured the journey he intended—a passage to another dimension. Even now, the sheer incredulity of it all hangs in the air, a gossamer thread spun from the fibers of disbelief.

I recounted the tale of Max Darcy's strange machinations that brought me here, and Jude Bailey's voice broke, laden with despair: "Does this mean we're trapped here eternally?"

I offered no reply, for the grim truth stood stark before us. Our fates were tethered to the whims of Max Darcy's research, a thread stretched thin over the chasm of time. When might he achieve the breakthrough required to free us? Human life is but a fleeting spark; perhaps his spark will extinguish before enlightenment dawns.

My palms were slick with anxiety when Steve Bond's voice cut through my thoughts, urgent and sharp: "Where is Rory? He vanished after leaping down!"

I met Steve Bond's gaze, "Do you know what happened to Rory?" I continued, "Rory, was found lifeless on the rooftop. He plummeted from a great height, yet landed on the rooftop as if gravity had rewritten its own rules."

Steve Bond flinched, the words striking him like a physical blow.

"Incredible as it seems," I pressed on, "he leapt from the balcony of a certain floor, yet ended his flight upon the rooftop. It defies reason, as though he soared upwards rather than downwards, to fall only after reaching some zenith—"

I halted, a revelation striking like a bolt of lightning. An absurd notion, yet its ridiculousness was the very key to the puzzle.

Steve Bond, perceptive as ever, sensed the shift in my demeanor. "What have you realized?" he demanded.

I inhaled deeply, grounding myself. "Time," I uttered, the word hanging portentously in the air.

Bewilderment clouded Jude Bailey and Steve Bond's eyes.

"The so-called 'other space,'" I elucidated, "is merely a realm where time diverges from our own. Do you grasp the implications?"

I shouted now, the urgency of epiphany driving my voice. "The elevator—a device manipulating the flow of time! In decelerating time, we traversed into another dimension, a continuum where time lags behind!"

Their confusion lingered, but I pressed on, "Einstein's relativity tells us that with time's dilation, spatial dimensions must stretch proportionally. Halve the speed of time, and a building's height doubles."

Steve Bond gasped, "So in the elevator—"

"Precisely!" I cut him off. "We were embedded within a time-slowing engine. Our perception lagged, accustomed as we are to temporal normalcy. Rising within this altered state, the building too ascended, its stature magnified in tandem with time's sluggish gait. Thus, our journey seemed interminable, culminating in our arrival in this altered dimension."

Steve Bond stammered, "And now—"

"We exist," I replied, "in a time-dilated space. To us, movement is routine, but from a normal time frame, we are phantoms moving in slow motion, our voices drawn out like a recording played at half speed."

Jude Bailey's face mirrored a dawning horror. "Then Rory—"

The complexity of my explanation unfurled slowly in their minds, and Steve Bond's question echoed with urgency: "Rory's death—how does it fit? The leap from balcony to rooftop defies logic!"

I drew a deep breath. "According to relativity, as time decelerates, spatial dimensions must expand. If time halved, the building's height would double, creating the illusion of a leap upwards."

Steve Bond and Jude Bailey's brows furrowed, grappling with the paradoxical nature of our predicament.

I waved my hand and continued, "This is a remarkable situation. In our space, the building has become taller, but in a normal space, the building remains its original height."

I paused for a moment, then added, "In two different spaces, everything is unimaginable."

Steve Bond and Jude Bailey remained silent, their brows furrowed.

I explained further, "Rory's situation is like this: he jumped down in a space where time slowed. As he descended, he suddenly broke through this space. When he did, he was still mid-air, but the building reverted to its original height. Consequently, he fell and landed on the rooftop."

Jude Bailey and Steve Bond took a deep breath. After a long moment, they slowly nodded.

An interminable silence followed. Steve Bond's lips curled into a bitter smile, a concession to the futility of their predicament. " So, under what conditions can we break through this space?"

The question hung in the air, resonating with the very answer I had been fervently seeking.

I paused, letting the gears of my mind whirl before responding, "It seems that Max Darcy's research has hit a wall. He managed to catapult us into this dimension where time drags its feet, but he hasn't figured out a way to bring us back."

Jude Bailey interjected abruptly, "But Rory made it out!"

Steve Bond's glare was sharp enough to cut glass. "Rory fell to his death," he snapped.

Jude Bailey's mouth moved silently, his expression screaming what he couldn't voice: Death might be preferable to an eternity trapped in this surreal limbo.

Steve Bond seemed poised to further chastise Jude Bailey, but amidst their brewing conflict, a realization began to crystallize in my mind. I gestured for them to quiet down, fearing their bickering would scatter my nascent thoughts.

Once serenity returned, I inhaled deeply. "Indeed, Rory breached this spatial prison; otherwise, he wouldn't have ended up on the rooftop."

Steve Bond shook his head, frustration etched into his features. "What's the point of such a breakthrough if it leads to death? I have no desire to meet the same fate."

I fixed my gaze on Steve Bond. "The critical question is: how much slower is time in this space we inhabit?"

"What difference does it make?" Steve Bond challenged.

"It makes all the difference," I countered. "If time here is halved, then metaphorically, a 300-foot building becomes 600 feet tall. Of course, the building's height remains constant for us, but for those in different time flows, it's drastically altered."

Both Steve Bond and Jude Bailey were rapt with attention.

I continued, "If we assume time is twice as slow , then jumping off here and breaching the spatial barrier as you descend is like leaping from 250 feet."

Steve Bond added somberly, "And if you land on the roof, that's one thing. But if you hit the ground, it's akin to falling from 550 feet." He gave a bitter smile. "No one survives a fall like that."

He was right. Such a descent is survivable only in fiction.

Jude Bailey spoke again, his voice brimming with reckless hope, "If only we had a parachute!"

Steve Bond shot him another icy glare, but I intervened. "Mr. Bailey, even with a parachute, it wouldn't help. You'd need the velocity of a rapid descent to puncture the barriers of this space. A parachute would only leave you floating in this decelerated void, a fate far worse."

Jude Bailey's hopeful expression wilted into a bitter smile. Steve Bond spread his hands in resignation. "So, we're out of options."

I paced the confines of the room, deep in thought, my brow furrowed with the weight of our dilemma. Then, with resolve hardening my voice, I declared, "I'm willing to take the risk."

Chapter 13

Journey Beyond the Fourth Dimension

Steve Bond's voice cut through the air like a knife, laden with disbelief and apprehension. "Have you lost your mind? This isn't some thrill-seeking escapade; it's a death wish!"

I met his gaze, my voice steady. "I'm not suggesting a blind leap to our doom. I have a plan, a way to increase our odds of survival."

Their faces were blank canvases of confusion, Steve Bond and Jude Bailey peering at me as if I had spoken in riddles. Steve Bond asked, incredulously, "And what, pray tell, could we possibly use here?"

I extended a finger, pointing toward a seemingly mundane object. Their eyes followed my gesture, landing on an unassuming door. From their bewildered expressions, it was clear they were still in the dark.

Steve Bond turned back to me, skepticism etched into his features. "What are you getting at?" he probed.

"The door," I replied simply.

Jude Bailey's brows knitted together, still grappling with the concept, but Steve Bond—ever the seasoned adventurer—caught on quickly.

"You mean, dismantle the door, use it as a makeshift shield, and descend with it?" he surmised, his voice tinged with the thrill of understanding.

I nodded. "Precisely. The door could cushion the impact, allowing me a shot at survival."

Jude Bailey glanced between us, struggling to reconcile this audacious scheme with reality. Yet Steve Bond, weighing the scant options, seemed to grasp its desperate logic.

Of course, the risk was monumental, the outcome uncertain. But as time ticked by, Steve Bond exhaled, and I had already moved to detach the door, preparing for the plunge.

I carved a handhold into the door with a knife, creating a grip to anchor myself during the fall.

With Steve Bond and Jude Bailey's help, I climbed higher, threading my arm through the aperture to clutch the door tightly.

I shook my head, a wry smile tugging at my lips. "Let's hope it holds up until I land."

Steve Bond offered a sardonic smile. "But you're heavier than the door, which means you'll hit the ground first and—"

"I know," I interrupted. "We'll need to weigh it down, ensure it lands first."

With an agile mind well-suited to this task, Steve Bond suggested, "Let's dismantle the wash basins!"

Nodding, we set about unscrewing the basins, affixing them beneath the door. Even then, it seemed insufficient, so we added a bathtub for good measure.

Together, we hefted the modified door, a bizarre contraption, towards the balcony railing.

Gazing at the amalgamation of wood, porcelain, and metal, a bitter laugh escaped me. Surely, no human in history had ever contemplated such a leap with such an apparatus.

Yet, in this otherworldly space, I wasn't alone. Steve Bond and Jude Bailey were my compatriots in this temporal anomaly, and who knew how many others languished in parallel dimensions?

I scaled the railing, the world below a dizzying abyss. As I stood perched on the edge, Steve Bond and Jude Bailey watched, tension etched on their faces. I embraced them in turn, a silent vow exchanged.

In that moment, I felt akin to a kamikaze pilot, steeling myself for the unknown.

I threaded my hand through the door's hold, securing my grip. "On my mark, push it out carefully, then release."

They nodded, and Jude Bailey, his voice quavering, asked, "What if you make it through?"

"If I do," I replied, "I'll find a way back, and we can all escape together."

Jude Bailey's face twisted with doubt. "It might work once, but not again."

Though I harbored disdain for his pessimism, I masked it with reassurance. "I'll return with better tools."

Steve Bond, ever more concerned for my safety than his own, simply said, "Goodbye," his voice thick with emotion.

"Goodbye," I echoed, and with that, they pushed.

Together, the door and I plummeted, gravity grabbing hold as the world blurred past.

The door's weighted bottom kept me upright, feet first, as I hurtled downward.

Having once been an avid skydiver, I was no stranger to freefall, but this was a different beast altogether. The velocity was such that I felt as though my very organs might burst forth.

It was a harrowing sensation, my body a tumult of nausea and vertigo. I clamped down on the urge to retch, focusing solely on the descent.

I was aware only of my descent, completely oblivious to the situation that awaited me, until my vision cleared, revealing the rooftop of a building rushing up to meet me.

As I glimpsed the rooftop looming closer, I estimated a hundred feet remained, but the ground rushed toward me with relentless speed, leaving no time for anything but a primal scream. A deafening crash accompanied the violent jolt as I landed atop the building.

Though the door had absorbed much of the impact, the force was still staggering. My senses reeled, the world spinning. I could vaguely hear the bathtub shattering, a cacophony of splintering wood signaling the door's disintegration.

The door, which I had clung to so desperately, was yanked apart by the impact, flinging me five or six feet across the rooftop. The fall was brutal, but the door had taken the brunt of it. With effort, I pushed against the ground, rising shakily to my feet.

The residual force sent me staggering back several steps before I could steady myself. Pain radiated through my body, yet triumph surged through me. I had made it! I had escaped the clutches of the time-dilated space.

Surveying the wreckage, I saw the bathtub and washbasins reduced to shards, the door fragmented into splinters. Somehow, amidst the destruction, I stood unscathed, the rooftop bearing a gaping wound from our collision.

Breathless, I took a step forward. Suddenly, the sound of an iron door creaked open, echoing from the elevator room that jutted out from the rooftop. A figure emerged, rounding the corner to meet my gaze. It was Max Darcy.

His expression was indescribable—eyes bulging, mouth agape, a strangled sound escaping his lips. The sight of me, emerging from the impossible, had left him paralyzed with shock.

I advanced slowly, voice level. "Surprised to see me? It seems my return is not quite the welcome you anticipated."

Max Darcy's composure slowly returned, though fear still colored his features. He stammered, "That—this can't be. How did you solve what I could not?"

I bore him no ill will. He had warned me of the risks, and my decision to face them was my own. "Rory inspired me," I explained. "You remember him, the administrator?"

Max Darcy nodded, confusion still clouding his eyes. "I still don't understand."

"You wouldn't," I replied, "because you haven't experienced that other space."

At the mention of "another space," Max Darcy recoiled, his face blanching. "You—know everything?"

I shook my head. "No, only fragments. Most is conjecture. The elevator, it's a time-slowing apparatus, isn't it?"

Max Darcy retreated, pressing against the elevator wall, his hands fluttering in agitation, words eluding him.

I stepped closer, relentless in my pursuit. "Passing through it thrusts individuals into a temporal anomaly. That's where I was, and how I returned, correct?"

His pallor deepened, yet finally, he nodded.

"In that realm, I encountered Jude Bailey and my friend Mr. Bond," I continued.

Max Darcy murmured, "I know. I saw you."

His words left me momentarily speechless. "You saw us? How?"

Max Darcy held my gaze, a bitter smile playing on his lips. "I suppose there's no point in hiding the truth now."

I couldn't suppress the edge in my voice. "You never should have hidden anything. We need to extract them from that space, and swiftly. Surely, you have a solution."

Max Darcy's demeanor grew weary, his hands rubbing his face as if to dispel fatigue. "Follow me," he said, turning away.

He led me around the elevator room's corner, and I followed. As we rounded the bend, I was met by another figure at the door—Dr. Harry.

Flora greeted me with a rueful smile. I grasped his hand, clapping a companionable hand on his shoulder, and together we followed Max Darcy inside.

Crossing the threshold, I was struck dumb by the sight before me.

This was no ordinary elevator machine room. The confined space bristled with an array of equipment reminiscent of Houston's Space Control Center, albeit on a much smaller scale. Instruments lined the walls, their myriad lights flickering in a ceaseless dance. The room was cramped, barely accommodating the three of us standing, let alone allowing any room to sit.

I maneuvered through the narrow aisle between the rows of devices, following Max Darcy. Once inside, his demeanor transformed. He was a different man here—his eyes sparkled with fervor, his face aglow with a pride that seemed to emanate from within, as if he were a fish reunited with water.

His voice was both firm and assured. "Be mindful of your hands. A single button pressed could alter the course of human history."

Despite the hyperbole, I believed him implicitly. I raised my hands above my head, turning sideways to carefully make my way through the tight space to join him, Flora trailing close behind.

Max Darcy and I stood before a small monitor, scarcely bigger than a human palm. "Watch closely," he instructed.

As I tried to decipher his meaning, Max Darcy and Flora sprang into action, fingers deftly manipulating the controls, hollering questions back and forth. After a brief flurry of activity, the screen flickered to life with a burst of erratic lines that gradually coalesced into a recognizable image—a vacant living room within this very building.

"This is the living room of a unit here," I said, puzzled. "Why are we watching it on a screen instead of just going there?"

Max Darcy shot me a stern glance, his confidence undiminished. "You wouldn't understand. Even I barely grasp the complexities of the fourth dimension, but at least listen."

I chuckled at the irony. "Appreciate the compliment."

Unfazed, Max Darcy continued, "The concept of another space is beyond imagination. When you were in that other realm, you were still physically here in this building, just in another space. People in different spaces can't perceive each other."

I nodded, understanding the basic premise. "I'm aware."

Max Darcy's tone turned didactic, like a professor schooling a novice. "Aware? Do you know the years of toil it took to enable radio waves to penetrate these parallel spaces?"

His words resonated with me, my heart quickening at the implications. "So, we can observe them on this screen?"

Max Darcy affirmed, "Yes."

He resumed pressing buttons, and I focused on the screen as images flickered and shifted. The view remained fixed on the building's unit halls until abruptly, a figure appeared. I shouted in recognition, prompting Max Darcy to halt.

As I watched the small screen, the image was clear, despite its size. In the corner sat Jude Bailey, his posture one of despair, head cradled in his hands. He was almost still, and when I turned to Max Darcy, he simply encouraged me to "Keep watching!"

I focused back on the screen as another figure entered— unmistakably Steve Bond. Though no larger than an inch on the display, his identity was clear. Yet, his movements were perplexing.

Steve Bond wasn't walking in the usual sense. His movements resembled a slow, deliberate dance, each hand and foot lifted with exaggerated care as he approached Jude Bailey.

Jude Bailey rose to meet him, matching Steve Bond's slow, graceful motions. It was akin to watching a film slowed to a crawl, where every action was drawn out, reminiscent of a slow-motion documentary capturing the intricacies of a 100-meter sprint, every sinew and muscle tremor meticulously detailed.

Max Darcy, standing beside me, provided an explanation. "Time flows ten times slower in that space. To us, their actions appear decelerated."

I glanced at him for further insight, and he continued, "Every process is slowed, even biological ones."

Considering this, I remarked, "Our priority is to bring them back. I believe a rapid descent could breach the spatial barrier."

Max Darcy studied me before responding, "Mr. Morris, you now know all there is to understand. I must ask for your discretion."

I withheld a promise, replying, "That depends on the circumstances."

"And your plan for retrieving them?" Max Darcy queried.

"I'll return, equipped to handle the dangers of high-altitude falls."

With a sigh, Max Darcy offered a compliment, "You possess great courage. I regret we didn't meet sooner."

Navigating the complex maze of machinery, I reassured him, "I'll keep your secret for now, but I'll prepare to extract them swiftly. May I use the elevator?"

He granted permission with a nod.

A question occurred to me. "Is the transition between spaces controlled entirely from here?"

Max Darcy exchanged a look with Flora before nodding once more. A flicker of anger surged within me, the impulse to lash out almost overwhelming.

But I held back. Violence would solve nothing. The situation was what it was, and blame would not alter it.

Sensing my frustration, Max Darcy offered a tired, understanding smile. "Mr. Morris, initially, it was an accident. Those who ventured into the other space could return, but then—something changed, unexpectedly—"

He left the sentence unfinished, but the implications were clear. The situation had spiraled beyond their control, a scientific venture now fraught with unforeseen complications. I resolved to focus on the task ahead, determined to bring Steve Bond and Jude Bailey back safely, despite the unknowns that lay ahead.

Chapter 14

Return to the Time-Slowed Space

Max Darcy seemed ready to explain further, but I interrupted him. "No more explanations. I don't have time for that," I stated with urgency in my voice.

He acknowledged my resolve with a nod. "Your focus should be on bringing them back."

I scrutinized him, my suspicion growing. "I want both of you to come with me upstairs."

Max Darcy's expression turned slightly regretful. "You don't trust me?"

"You could say that," I replied, my tone cool and steady. "I need to secure my own safety. If I can't return from the slowed-time space, none of us will, and your secretive operations will remain buried."

My straightforward words seemed to sting, leaving Max Darcy flushed with a mix of anger and defensiveness. "I'm not concealing anything out of shame. My work is about transforming human history and civilization. It's a grand 'enterprise'!" he declared, his voice filled with passion.

I regarded him with a cold, detached gaze. "Then why all the secrecy? Why the hidden identity?"

His earlier defiance faded, replaced by a quieter tone. "It wasn't my choice, not my idea."

"Then whose idea was it?" I pressed, my eyes locked onto his.

Max Darcy fell silent, as if paralyzed by the question. I turned to Flora, hoping for some revelation, but he too looked back at Max Darcy, evidently as clueless and expectant as I was.

Without offering a response, Max Darcy gestured tiredly. "Harry, let's escort Mr. Morris down."

Flora, following Max Darcy's direction like a puppet, moved to comply.

We left the control room, traversed the rooftop, and began to descend a flight of stairs. The atmosphere was tense, filled with unspoken questions and unresolved issues. As we walked, I remained alert and focused, knowing that understanding the full extent of Max Darcy's intentions—and ensuring a safe return—was crucial.

Upon reaching the 23rd floor, Flora's sudden remark caught me off guard. "They're on the 23rd floor."

The realization hit me like a jolt. "You knew which floor we were on?"

Flora glanced at Max Darcy, then confirmed, "Yes, you were all on the 23rd floor."

We were heading toward the elevator, but his revelation stopped me in my tracks. I turned abruptly and forcefully opened the door to a residential unit.

My breath came in rapid gasps, anxiety clawing at my chest.

From behind, Max Darcy cautioned, "Mr. Morris, even though we're on the same floor, remember we exist in separate spaces."

I scanned the empty room, its silence a taunting void. I turned back, exhaling sharply. "Mr. Darcy, I have a question."

He seemed to anticipate it. "I know what you're going to ask."

I met his gaze, and he admitted, "You want to know if the bathtub, washbasin, and door you dismantled are still here?"

I nodded, eyes fixed on him. Max Darcy rubbed his face thoughtfully. "Theoretically, they've been removed. You can verify for yourself."

An inexplicable sense of mystery enveloped me as I ventured further inside. Down a short corridor, I found a room without a door.

My heart thundered in my chest. Without hesitation, I rushed to the bathroom. As expected, the bathtub and washbasin were absent.

I spun around, seized by a wild idea. This was the apartment unit. Steve Bond and Jude Bailey were here! I called out their names, desperation mounting as I dashed through the hall.

Madness gripped me. I couldn't comprehend why I couldn't see, touch, or hear them when every instinct insisted they were present.

Without the scientific expertise to unravel temporal and spatial anomalies, I struggled to reconcile what was happening. I could only accept the premise, however reluctantly. The reality of separate spaces on the same floor was confounding, yet undeniable. Each unanswered question only fueled my determination to bridge the gap and bring them back.

Emotion overwhelmed reason as I shouted and flailed, striking walls and doors, driven by the irrational hope that my friends would emerge from their unseen refuge.

Max Darcy and Flora rushed in to restrain me, and finally, their grip brought me to a standstill, breathless and agitated.

Max Darcy's voice cut through my turmoil. "You know this won't work. Why persist?"

Shrugging them off, I advanced on Max Darcy, finger accusatory. "Max Darcy, you're not human. You're a devil!"

My accusation was harsh, and Max Darcy's face darkened with its weight.

Yet he remained composed, meeting my gaze steadily. "Yes, call me a devil. Will you bind me and set me ablaze?"

His unexpected retort left me dumbstruck.

Slowly, my accusatory finger dropped.

When I lashed out at him, I felt justified, but his response quickly deflated my anger.

Who was I to judge someone like him? Max Darcy was a visionary, a pioneer in his field, capable of transcending the boundaries of our known universe by sending people into alternate dimensions. Such achievements are inherently unsettling, yet every groundbreaking scientific discovery has been met with skepticism and fear. History is littered with tales of trailblazing scientists who were persecuted for their ideas.

I lowered my hand, my rage giving way to a quiet apology. "I'm sorry."

He said nothing, his face remaining a mask of resignation.

"I truly am," I repeated, seeking to convey the sincerity of my apology.

Max Darcy placed a hand on my shoulder, a faint smile breaking through his stoic exterior. "Forget it. I think you're starting to understand me. You might be the one who understands me best someday."

I offered a wry smile in return. "We need to focus on rescuing Jude Bailey and Steve Bond. I hope you won't stand in my way."

"I won't stop you," Max Darcy assured me, though his voice carried a note of deep sadness. "It's not me who insists on keeping my work a secret."

I could empathize with his burden, so I patted his shoulder reassuringly. "Don't worry. I'll find a way to resolve this. Trust me."

With a sigh, he accompanied me out of the unit and into the elevator. I noticed the elevator's interior was pristine, repaired since I had last dismantled parts of it. As we descended, I inquired, "There was an instance where Steve Bond made a phone call between two spaces. How did that happen?"

Max Darcy shook his head. "I'm not entirely sure. It likely occurs when the barrier between spaces is at its weakest. My theory involves decelerating radio waves to slow the speed of light and manipulate time. But radio waves are subject to interference—both cosmic and terrestrial."

He paused, reflecting on the limitations of human endeavors. "Humans are minuscule in the grand scheme. Despite our efforts, we're constantly hindered by natural and artificial interferences."

Silent, I stepped out of the elevator as it reached the lobby.

Max Darcy queried, "How do you plan to rescue them? Your escape was a stroke of luck."

I shook my head. "It wasn't luck; it was ingenuity. I'll devise a method, as long as you can send me back."

With a bitter smile, he nodded.

I departed, Max Darcy and Flora bidding farewell at the building's entrance.

Once home, Flora immediately questioned my whereabouts. Upon recounting my ordeal, even she, typically unflappable, was momentarily speechless.

"What's your next move?" she asked, though her expression revealed she already knew my intent.

Taking her hand, I replied, "I have no choice but to go back."

Flora, after a pause, nodded. "Yes, you have no other option, but—"

I shared her concerns. This wasn't a typical adventure; it involved traversing into an unpredictable dimension, beyond human control. My first return was due to rapid descent, but there was no guarantee of repeating that success.

I took a deep breath. "Even if I can't return immediately, I'll eventually find a way back. You might be an old woman by then," I joked, trying to lighten the mood.

Flora, despite her worries, managed a calm exterior. "This is like 'seven days in the mountains, a thousand years in the world'."

I nodded, acknowledging the ancient perspective.

Understanding different dimensions and time flows is a complex concept, even for modern minds. Yet, such ideas aren't new. The tale of "Lancle Mountain" tells of a woodcutter entering another realm.

Pacing, I continued, "That's the worst-case scenario. Realistically, I believe it's manageable. I'll prepare three parachutes and three bags of lead for safety. It's risky, but far safer than clutching a door."

Flora simply nodded, offering her silent support.

I called Colonel Jack, the only one who could supply what I needed promptly. I didn't share my full story, considering Max Darcy and Flora were possibly under external pressure. Publicizing the matter could jeopardize them both.

I requested the necessary items from Colonel Jack. He agreed but was puzzled. "Your request is contradictory—a parachute slows descent, but lead accelerates it. What are you planning?" he asked.

"It's a bit complicated," I replied to Colonel Jack with a half-joking remark, " Colonel, your grasp of scientific principles is truly lacking. Surely you've heard of the Leaning Tower of Pisa experiment? Whether you fall with or without a 100-pound lead block, your descent speed remains the same." I imagined Colonel Jack on the other end, caught off guard by my jest, his response a jumble of words.

After setting a time for him to deliver the items, I ended the call. The three 100-pound lead bags were to stabilize our descent, not to hasten it. They were meant to ensure we landed precisely and not drift into unknown territories.

With everything arranged, I sat down with Flora across from me. We sat in silence, the weight of the task ahead heavy in the room.

Colonel Jack's efficiency was impressive. In just an hour, he arrived with the supplies I'd requested. Flora insisted on accompanying me to the building, and I couldn't bring myself to refuse her. Together, we drove to the site.

Upon arriving, we found Max Darcy and Flora waiting at the entrance. As we stepped out, I noticed Max Darcy's uneasy glance at Flora. I reassured him, "Mr. Darcy, rest assured, she won't speak a word of this, even if I don't return."

Max Darcy offered a weak smile. The three of us unloaded the equipment from the car and carried it into the lobby, heading for the elevator.

As the elevator doors slid open, Flora and I exchanged a deep breath.

"You've been there once. Let me go this time," Flora suggested.

I forced a smile. "Do you think this is a picnic?"

She sighed, "No."

We loaded the lead weights and parachutes into the elevator. Facing the trio outside, I could see their nervousness mirrored my own.

"Don't worry. If all goes as planned, I'll be back in half an hour," I assured them. Then I added, "Of course, that's the time here."

With that, the elevator doors closed. I watched the row of lights above the door. They lit up as the elevator began its ascent, then faded to darkness.

Understanding dawned on me. Time would slow as the elevator climbed, a testament to Max Darcy's pioneering work. His research was groundbreaking, yet incomplete. Ideally, I would ascend to the time-slowed space and return through the same elevator to normal time.

As the elevator continued its ascent, I felt surprisingly calm. The wait was long, but this time I was prepared, mentally bracing for the journey into the unknown.

When the elevator finally halted and the doors parted, I let out a triumphant shout. Steve Bond and Jude Bailey burst forth, their expressions a mixture of disbelief and relief. Jude Bailey paused, stunned to see me, while Steve Bond, with unexpected vigor, turned and punched Jude Bailey. "What did I say? Ash Morris would come back, you fool," he exclaimed.

Jude Bailey took the blow silently, and I quickly intervened. "Enough, stop fighting. Let's get these things out!"

We worked swiftly, unloading the elevator and moving the supplies into the unit. As we did, I succinctly recounted the events of my previous jump, ensuring they grasped the urgency and gravity of our situation.

"There's no point in staying here longer than necessary," I urged. "Let's get ready and put on the parachutes."

Jude Bailey struggled with the parachute, clearly unused to the equipment. I guided him through the process, and together, carrying the lead weights, we made our way to the balcony.

Nerves were apparent; Jude Bailey's face was pale, and perspiration beaded on Steve Bond's forehead. We climbed over the railing, and I adopted a commanding demeanor, like a general leading his troops into battle.

"Follow my lead. Once we spot the rooftop, I'll give the command to release. Let go of the lead first, then deploy the parachutes. Aim to land on the rooftop, so be cautious about opening the parachute too early. Got it?"

Both nodded, and I prepared us for the leap. "Jump!" I shouted, and we plunged into the void together. Unlike my previous descent, this time I felt more in control, unencumbered by obstacles.

The world blurred as we fell, and then the rooftop came into view, the descent swiftly accelerating. "Release!" I hollered.

In unison, we released the lead bags, watching them plummet. We deployed our parachutes just in time, mere feet from the rooftop. One lead bag struck the elevator room, crashing through the roof and triggering an explosion that sent flames leaping skyward.

By the time the fire erupted, we had landed safely.

I quickly disentangled myself from the parachute cords and raced to the machine room's door, but thick smoke billowed from the cracks. Flames engulfed the interior, forcing us to retreat. We dashed to the elevator, only to find smoke seeping from its doors as well. "Down the stairs, quickly!" I yelled.

As we raced down the stairs, the smoke enveloped us faster than we could descend. By the time we reached the final floors, we were engulfed in a thick, choking haze.

Bursting into the lobby, we sprinted toward the exit. Outside, I spotted Flora waiting by the car. I called out, and she quickly joined us, her eyes wide with concern as smoke billowed from the building's every crevice.

"Where are they?" I demanded, anxiety tightening my voice.

Flora, taken aback, replied, "They're in the elevator machine room on the rooftop. Didn't you see them?"

Her words sent a chill through me. I spun around, but it was too late. Flames now consumed the building, and I knew Max Darcy and Flora's chances of survival were bleak.

Three days after the fire reduced the building to a skeletal husk, Steve Bond and I returned. Firefighters were still sifting through the remnants. We stood silently, grappling with the reality that no bodies had been found. If Max Darcy and Flora had been in the computer room during the blaze, they wouldn't have stood a chance.

Doubts gnawed at me—was the fire an unintended consequence of the lead piercing the computer room's roof, or had it been a deliberate act by Max Darcy? The question haunted me, yet the answer remained elusive.

The identity of the true mastermind behind Max Darcy's work remained shrouded in mystery. Despite several encounters with "Shark," he consistently feigned ignorance, leaving no openings for further inquiry. I chose not to press him, sensing that any attempt would be futile and potentially dangerous.

As time passed, the building that had been the epicenter of these strange events was demolished, its remnants swept away. Yet, the mysteries that had unfolded within its walls lingered, unresolved and enigmatic, whispering questions into the void that would likely never be answered.

Though the physical structure was gone, the experiences and the unanswered questions left a lasting impression on those of us who had been involved.

The secrets of alternate spaces, the fate of Max Darcy and Flora, and the true intentions behind their experiments remained topics of silent contemplation, mysteries that lay beyond the reach of the known world.

In the end, the story of that building and its secrets faded into obscurity, a curious footnote in the annals of time. But for those who had been touched by its mysteries, it was a reminder of the vast unknowns that still lie beyond human understanding, waiting perhaps for another brave soul to uncover them.

www.ingramcontent.com/pod-product-compliance
Lightning Source LLC
Chambersburg PA
CBHW031558310726
48974CB00003B/715